# LAIRD OF SHADOWS

## A MACDOUGALL LEGACY NOVEL

### ELIZA KNIGHT

KNIGHT
MEDIA

*When darkness falls... Only true love can save them...*

Beiste MacDougall has only just found himself as laird of his clan after a brutal attack from Vikings leaves his father slain. On the night of his sire's death, a beautiful woman comes to his castle begging for help, calling upon a vow their clans had made years before. Though he'd rather wallow in his pain, Beiste is tempted by the lass, the secrets she holds, and the chance at retribution she brings.

Lady Elle Cam'béal is desperate to save her brother and her clan from the vile clutches of her Viking enemies. But there is only one man who can help her, a handsome, provocative laird with a beastly temper. When he locks her in a chamber, she is visited by an apparition, and left with a secret that changes her destiny. Elle must figure out a way to accept her fate, but also forge a future of her own choosing.

As battles and treachery rain down upon them, Beiste and Elle find unlikely allies in each other, and a few stolen moments of passion that bring light from the shadows...

∼

SECOND EDITION

FEBRUARY 2017

Copyright 2016 © Eliza Knight

Edited by: Scott Moreland

***This is the extended novel version of the original novella published in September 2016 in the Once Upon a Haunted Castle anthology.

❀ Created with Vellum

*To my own knight, who comforts me whenever I have a ghostly dream...*

## ACKNOWLEDGMENTS

Thank you so very much to my amazing writing partners, Ruth, Madeline, Kathryn and Terri! Without you all, this book would not have been possible. And what a blast it was writing! Thank you to my traveling partners in crime, Andrea Snider and Brenna Ash who visited Dunstaffnage with me!

Dear Reader,

I'm thrilled to introduce you to my new series, The MacDougall Legacy. Legends abound within the stories, and many with a mystical element. Laird of Shadows, is sort of like my own twisted fairy tale version of *Beauty and the Beast*. Elle's name means beauty, and Beiste is a Scottish name for Beast.

The history of Scotland is seeped in mysticism, and so most of the elements I've added into this series are based on historical fact or legend.

For example, there is the legend of the Green Lady at Dunstaffnage Castle—a *glaistig*, which I've used in my story here, *Laird of Shadows*. You will also find that in history, Castle Campbell was called Castle Gloom, and the nearby trickling stream was the Burn of Sorrows. Considering the devastation that befalls my characters, it is only fitting.

I do hope you enjoy the stories and that you continue to follow the MacDougall family throughout the series.

Cheers and Happy Reading!
    Eliza

astle Gloom
*Scottish Highlands*
*1207*

THEY'D NEVER SURVIVE.

Elle Cam'béal stared deep into her mother's widened gaze. In the lady's solar, they'd been mending shirts for her father's warriors. But the *leines* and threaded needles dropped to their laps, forgotten now.

"What was that?" Elle asked, fear prickling along the nape of her neck. Every hair on her arms and the back of her neck stood on end.

Her mother, Lady Amma Cam'béal, swallowed, eyes flying toward Elle's younger brother Erik who appeared quite engrossed in the text his tutor had left him to study.

"A horn," her mother finally answered. She blinked. Her mouth opening and closing. Her gaze shifting toward the window and then back to her children.

"I heard it." Elle stood, walking toward the window, but

her mother's hurried steps followed, her fingers reached out, grasping Elle's arm, stilling her.

Amma's face had paled, her fingertips cold against Elle's skin. "Do not go to the window. Elle, ye must listen to me. Stay away from the window. Take your brother. Hide him."

"Hide him?" Elle shook her head in confusion. "Mama, please, tell me what is happening."

"They have come for me. For ye." The ominous words sent a shiver of dread up Elle's spine.

"Who? Who has come?" Panic seized Elle, constricting her chest. The two maids who'd been in the chamber with them also dropped their sewing, their hands clasped in fear.

Lady Amma was a great warrior—if she was scared, that meant they truly did have much to fear.

Erik set down his leather-bound text, his young eyes studying them in their sudden dread. "What's going on?"

"Erik, ye must go with Elle. The two of ye need to hide. I will tell them…" But her mother's voice trailed off as she licked at her dry lips, her hands wringing before her. "I will tell them that ye've married, Elle, and that Erik is fostering out. That ye are both gone away from here."

"What?" Elle fisted her hands at her sides, wanting to grab her mother by the shoulders, give her a shake, and demand to know what was happening. Married? Aye, she was of marriageable age, and Erik was certainly of an age to foster… But why should they have to lie? Who was coming? Who could be so dangerous?

The horn sounded again. An eerie moan that filled every corner, brought to life every shadow. The sound sank into Elle's bones, vibrating her insides and making her knees go weak.

"I know that sound," Erik said. "That is the horns of your family, is it not, Mama?"

Her family… *Vikings.*

Amma wanting them to run made sense now. She feared they were all doomed. And with good reason.

Their mother's throat bobbed as she swallowed and gave a near imperceptible nod. "Ye must hide. Now. If they catch ye..." She trailed off, not ready to explain the whole of her thoughts. Then she shook her head, grasping tightly to Elle's hands. "Dinna hide, daughter. Run. Run far away. Run to the MacDougall."

Erik raised a fisted hand to the sky. "Never! I shall fight!"

"Erik, ye dinna understand," Mother said, her voice filling with anguish. "My family believes me a traitor. These lands were meant for them. We took them. This day… it has been a long time coming. They will not hesitate…to kill ye Erik. Ye must remain alive. Ye must protect your sister."

Erik glanced at Elle, sudden pride in his features. He puffed his ten summers old chest. "As ye wish."

"I wish it. I demand it." Mother reached for them both, pulling them into a fierce hug.

Elle tried to force herself to quell her shaking, if only to show her mother she could be strong. The door to the solar burst open and father's stout frame filled the doorway. Padrig Cam'béal had a shock of red hair, a testament to his Irish roots. Years ago, he'd served a Scottish laird—the MacDougall—who'd given him this castle and the lands, in exchange for his sword and fealty.

"Amma…" Father ground out. "Take the children. Ye must go. Bjork has come."

Mother nodded. "I know. We heard the horns. But I will not leave ye here to fight alone. Bjork is here because of me. The children will go. We will fight Bjork together."

Padrig tried to argue, but Amma would hear nothing of it. She was a warrior in her own right, and did not shy from a battle. In fact, Elle had seen her mother ride out, sword held high, to fight off neighboring clans who raided their lands.

For Amma to run would go against everything she prided herself on.

But Padrig was not through arguing with his wife. He pulled Amma aside, their fierce whispers echoing with the sounds of the horn and men from below the window preparing for the impending siege.

The two maids shifted toward the door then scurried out, no doubt preparing to gather their loved ones and hide, too.

At long last, Amma and Padrig embraced, a kiss that mingled with their tears. Elle shivered and held tight to Erik's hand, only sheer force of will keeping her own tears at bay. She glanced down at her brother. She would keep him safe. Until her dying day, this lad would be safe.

"Mama? Da?" Elle said.

Her parents pulled apart, the anguish on their face enough to pull those stubborn tears from Elle. They did not expect to see her or Erik again. That much was evident on their faces. This was going to be a fight to the death.

What was Elle to make of that? How was she to deal with it? They were a close-knit family. They were the reason she'd not yet wanted to wed, not wanting to leave them. Elle feared her own face mirrored their stricken expressions and worked quickly to clear her face of any and all emotion. This was not the end. They would see each other again. As soon as her parents vanquished Bjork and his band of marauding Vikings.

"Hug Mama and Da," she instructed Erik. "We shall be seeing them very shortly."

Erik hugged his parents tight and then Elle. As her father wrapped his burly arms around her, he said, "Take the sword from the hearth."

"*The* sword?" Elle blanched.

Padrig nodded, his face solemn. "Ye know of what I speak, lass. I canna risk Bjork getting his hands on it."

And she did understand. The massive claymore hung above the hearth in their great hall. A gift from Laird MacDougall. A promise. An oath. A secret engrained deep in the stones and the blood of many.

"The MacDougall, and that sword, will keep the both of ye safe."

Elle nodded. Her father touched her cheek, his fingers trembling slightly.

"Go now." Their mother ushered them out of her solar. "Go afore it's too late."

Elle took Erik's hand as they shuffled down the hall, dread in her belly and the sound of the Viking horns putting her more than a little on edge.

"Grab your cloak." Elle stopped outside of Erik's small chamber, just across the corridor from her own. "I'm going to get mine." They parted ways, even those brief moments filling her with panic when she could no longer see him.

*Hurry.* She opened her wardrobe, grabbing her cloak and the small dagger she often used when hunting. She tucked the dagger in her belt loop and then stooped to change from her impractical slippers to her boots.

"I'm ready," Erik said from the entrance.

"Help me with the laces."

Erik hurried forward, tying one of her boots while she tied the other. As soon as they were done, they rushed down to the great hall, which was oddly empty and quiet of servants. The candles had been extinguished, and the only light came from the hearth. With no windows, the chamber was dark and bouncing with shadows.

After blowing out the light that would only aid the Vikings in their raid, the servants had no doubt rushed off to hide. A thing that she and Erik needed to do now.

Elle dragged her father's overlarge chair to the hearth, stood on its cushioned seat and lifted the massive claymore from where it had graced their hall for nearly a decade. The baldric with the Cam'béal crest on one strap of leather and the MacDougall on the other was also there. She strapped it on and Erik helped her to get the sword into the leather strappings. The weapon was massive, its tip nearly reaching the ground behind her.

"To the kitchens," she instructed.

Once there, they found a scullion cowering in the corner, and an older lad who Elle recognized as the scullion's brother. An idea came to her.

"Ye there," she said to the lad. "I need ye to run as fast as ye can to MacDougall."

"Dunstaffnage Castle?" the lad asked, looking skeptical.

"Aye. Ye go and run along. Tell him we're under siege and to bring a legion of men to help us. Tell him the Vikings have come."

This only made the wee lass sob more.

"My sister..." the lad started, warring between duty to family and duty to his mistress. His face was filled with all the torment Elle would have felt had she to make the same choice.

"We will take her with us," Elle said. "Go. Hurry."

The lad rushed through the rear door without looking back.

"Stop that blubbering at once," Elle said, knowing she was being harsh. She reached a hand out to the girl, her actions softening her rebuke. "Your brother expects ye to be alive when he returns. And the only way that's going to happen is if ye stand up and dry your tears. Come with us and we shall see ye safe."

Just when Elle was certain the lass was not going to listen and instead continue to cry until the Vikings broke through the castle's foundation, she slowly stood. The wee thing couldn't be more than Erik's age.

"That's a good lass," Elle murmured. "What is your name?"

"Mary."

"All right, Mary. Let us go now."

The Vikings would search every inch of the castle. As her mother had said, there was no use trying to find a hiding spot inside, unless she wanted to be found. Their only choice was to run. The longer it took them to get out of the castle, the more chances they had of being caught. She prayed her Nordic relations could not break through her parents' defenses.

Elle stuffed a sack full of bannocks that had been abandoned while they cooled, and then gripping a child's hand on either side, she rushed out of the kitchen doors in much the same way her messenger had. They ran through the herbal gardens, past the chickens and toward the postern gate.

Outside, the sound of the approaching Vikings was even louder than it had been inside. Battle echoes waged from the front of the castle, seeming to reverberate from the sky. Cries of anguish, calls for mercy, and none given.

Elle's heart pounded behind her ribs as they crashed against the back wall and looked up at the top of the postern gate to a sentry who stood there, dread etched into the lines of his face. He nodded down to them. "I'll open the gate. Ye go! Now!"

Elle twisted the handle, pushing open the gate to freedom and fear. But that terror made the wee lass panic. Instead of running out the postern gate, Mary ran back toward the castle.

"Nay! Come back!" Elle shouted, but Mary did not cease her running.

"Go now, my lady," shouted the guard. "They are climbing the walls at the front of the castle. She is lost to ye. Protect Master Erik."

The pathway to freedom lay right before her, but Elle could not let the child die. Not when she'd promised the lad she'd take care of her if he'd run ahead with the message.

Elle grabbed her brother by the shoulders. "Run to the Burn of Sorrows." She thrust the bag of bannocks into his hands. "Hide where the rocks form a triquetra. I will meet ye there." She glanced up at the sentry. "Guard his back." The warrior nodded, knocking his arrow as his hardened stare followed Erik through the gate.

She didn't waste a moment watching him go, knowing the guard would shoot anyone who came near. Elle rushed back through the gardens, toward the side of the castle where she'd seen the girl round the corner. The guard was right. Vikings poured over the walls of the inner bailey. Smoke filled the air from burning arrows that sailed into bales of hay and anything that would catch fire—including men.

She pulled her hood over her head to hide her features and some of the carnage from view. Slinking against the edge of the castle wall, her hands shook as she touched them to the stones to steady herself.

At the end, hidden behind a stack of barrels, she caught sight Mary and grabbed hold of her. Tears tracked Mary's face, and she pointed through a space in the barrels to the center of the bailey.

Elle's blood ran cold, and she trembled harder, squeezing tight to the younger lass' shoulders as she followed the line of her finger. Her knees knocked together. Heart throbbed. Breath left her. Pain centered in her gut, and the only thing she could do was force herself to remain standing. To not give up. To be silent. To not call attention to herself. Slowly, she held her fingers to Mary's lips and whispered, "Shh..."

A man, larger than a tower himself, head partially shaved, long hanks of hair braided and black tar smeared over his features, took a jagged sword and thrust it through her father's chest. Laird Padrig Cam'béal reached out, as if to grab hold of his assailant for balance as his knees buckled. The Viking shoved her father to ground with a massive, bloodied boot, a vicious snarl on his face.

At once, Elle knew who the monster was—Bjork.

The brutal bastard left his sword in her father's chest and let out an evil battle cry. A cry of devilish victory.

Elle jerked Mary back toward her chest. "We must go," she whispered, urgent.

And just when they were about to turn away, Elle's mother came charging toward Bjork. Beautiful, ethereal, and full of ferocity. Her dark hair flew out behind her like raven's wings. She swung her sword with might and skill, the sun catching on its steel length. It all looked so ethereal. A nightmare of epic proportions. Bjork blocked every mighty blow, finally knocking her mother to the ground with a shake of his head and a snarl.

Elle stood stone still, her eyes wide, breath ceased, heart pounding so loud every other noise was drowned out. Her fingers went numb, even when Mary gripped her hand and tried to tug her away, she didn't feel it.

Bjork laughed as her mother struggled to stand, and he knocked her back down again. Blood poured from a laceration on Amma's smooth forehead. Elle sighed a breath of relief when Bjork walked away from her, leaving her alive. But that feeling of relief was too short lived, for he'd only turned around in order to pick up a large stone that had fallen from the wall...

*Nay. Nay. Nay.*

She wanted to scream. To run to her mother's rescue, but she knew to do so would only be to invite her own death. To invite Erik's death. And Mary's. Elle had made promises.

Elle turned then, dragging the lass with her, squeezing

her eyes shut, hoping to keep the sounds at bay as Bjork brought the stone down on her mother's skull. Though the blood rushed through her ears, and the resonances of battle raged, she swore she could hear the sound of her mother's bones splintering.

"I'm sorry," Mary sobbed.

"Ye did nothing."

"I ran. Ye laid witness to this because of me."

Laid witness... to her mother and father's death. They were gone.

There would be no more singing, sewing, laughing. No more games in the great hall, or feasts with their people. No more would she hug them. Elle stilled, her feet numb. Her knees threatened to buckle. They'd come out of the hiding place behind a barrel. Too exposed. A Viking leapt from the wall, loping toward them with vicious intent. An arrow from a guard upon the wall stopped him.

"Where is Lord Erik?" Mary shook Elle's arm.

"He..." Elle couldn't speak, her gaze riveted on the dead man before her. "The gate."

"I will take ye."

Seeming to realize that Elle needed her, the lass dragged her back around the side of the castle and toward the postern gate. The guards atop were no longer there, Elle suspected they'd gone to the front to help the warriors fighting there.

The two of them peered through the gate opening. It was now or never. No one approached. No one appeared to be there at all. "Come on," Elle said in hushed tones, the need to survive, to find Erik, jarring her from her stupor.

Their feet pounded over the grass toward the woods and the trickling waters of the Burn of Sorrow. In her mind, a hundred Bjorks followed close behind, but every time she turned around, no one was there.

They raced along the edges of the burn until their sides

seared with cramps and with every breath, bile threatened to expel, but still they ran. Finally, they reached the triquetra, about a half-mile from the castle. Erik lurched out at them, a rock in his hand, which only brought back thoughts of her mother. She couldn't tell him. Not now.

"'Tis only us. We must run," Elle said, relief making her feel faint at the sight of her brother. Despite the burning in her muscles, the ache in her heart, she pushed on.

A mile or so later, Mary begged to stop a moment and Elle relented, afraid if she didn't, they would all collapse. "A minute."

The two youngsters dropped to the ground, breathing hard. From a distance, she imagined the sounds of the battle still raged. They were not a safe distance yet. They had to keep going.

Elle leaned against a tree, her hand touching metal. A hunter's spike. "Wait here," she murmured, taking the heavy claymore from her back and setting it on the ground. She grabbed hold of the spikes and climbed up to the very top of the tree, catching view Castle Gloom.

What she saw left her shaken, trembling. Thick, black smoke curled skyward, mingling with the clouds. The Vikings had set fire to the castle. Which meant they knew she and Erik weren't there. Or they hoped to trap them inside. Either way, they'd soon realize they'd escaped and would come for them.

A gurgling noise came from her throat. She was going to be sick.

Elle turned her head, dry-heaving over leaves and, thankful nothing actually came up.

"Strength, Elle," she whispered to herself. "Strength."

How was she to gather this strength?

How was she to make it all the way to MacDougall lands with two young charges? The trip would take at least three days if they hurried. But likely more with the little ones unable to keep a grueling pace.

Sweet merciful heavens. She had to get back to her charges. Before the brutal murderers gave chase, if they hadn't already.

Elle made her way down the tree, strapped on the claymore and worked to keep her face blank of emotion, not wanting to worry them. Not wanting to tell them of the fire. The absolute destruction of all they knew. She sipped water from the burn with shaking hands. Erik and Mary followed suit, glancing at her from the sides of their eyes. The children didn't need to be told it was time to go, they waited expectantly for her to make the first move.

They ran until their lungs gave out, and then walked until they were able to run some more. Back and forth for another two hours, they rushed over the heath and through the wood, before coming across a small tenant farm and climbing over the short stone wall the farmer had built to keep his sheep inside.

Hurrying over the field, a small croft loomed up a the edges of their blurred vision, and the crofter stepped directly in their path. Large and foreboding, he held an iron ax in his thick hands.

"Where are ye off to?" He looked them up and down, suspicion on every line of his features and his dark brown eyes.

Elle bent over, hands on her knees, and breathed deep before standing up to face the man. The crofter was right to be suspicious. A woman, running at break neck speed with two children, was an unusual thing.

Elle worked to catch her breath. "We…" Saints but it was hard to speak with her lungs so tight. "Vikings… We escaped…"

"Vikings?" The crofter scratched his head, setting a foot up on the pile of wood he'd been chopping. "So far inland?"

Elle dragged in a gulp of air, worked to stand up straight. "They came for my parents."

He narrowed his eyes, flicked them over Erik and Mary. "Who might your parents be?"

This was where Elle hesitated. Should she tell the crofter? He would either offer them help, a horse perhaps, or rush them away. She prayed for Erik's sake it was the former. "Laird and Lady Cam'béal."

The crofter sucked in a breath staring behind her, perhaps expecting to see a bunch of wild warriors leaping through the edge of the forest. He scrubbed a meaty hand over his dark beard. "I see. Ye best come inside then."

Elle shook her head, fearing that the stranger would likely hand them over at the first sign of trouble. All she wanted was a horse. They were still on MacDougall lands, but that did not mean a crofter would be willing to give his freedom for theirs. She was about to tell him no thank ye, when a gentle-looking woman came outside, wiping her hands on an apron. As soon as the woman spotted them she looked to her husband, worry on her face.

"What's going on, Barra?"

"Castle's under siege. These are the laird's children."

Elle did not correct him if it would help Mary to be labeled with them. Erik and Mary, too, kept quiet.

"Oh, saints preserve us. Come inside," the woman rushed, waving her arms toward them. "Hurry."

"We'll keep ye safe. I promise," Barra said, his grip tightening on the ax. "Your Da has done much for us. We owe him our lives."

Elle couldn't explain it, but she did feel more comfortable, safer. Perhaps it wouldn't be a bad idea to rest inside for a little bit before they set out again.

Erik and Mary looked at her with worry, and at her nod, relaxed. They followed Barra and his wife inside. The croft was warm, a fire lit in the hearth and something burbled in the cauldron hanging over the flames. There was only one tiny window, open slightly to let out the smoke. A table was covered in the makings of a basket being woven and vegetables that needed chopping.

A small, sunken bed was against the far wall, and a loft above held many of the crofter's supplies. A pig snorted in the corner and a couple of chickens pecked at the dirt floor.

"Please, dinna mind the mess, my lady," Barra's wife said, sweeping a hand over the blanket on the bed and indicating they should sit.

"We dinna mind at all." Elle pushed the two young ones to sit by the bed and she pulled a stool from before the hearth to sit near them.

"I'm going to warn the other crofters." Barra nodded to Elle and kissed his wife. "Bar the door."

Barra's wife, Glenna she told them, served them each a bowl of stew, some weak, warm ale, and a hunk of dry brown bread. They ate in silence, though every bite was a struggle since she had no appetite. Not knowing when her next meal would come, she worked to force it down. Besides, Elle was glad to not have to talk about the siege, or the death of her parents. The pain was still too fresh, and every other bite, she nearly choked from her heart rushing to her throat.

Glenna didn't ask any questions, though she glanced at them with sympathy more than once. 'Twas for the best she didn't ask. The less Glenna knew, the less the Vikings could ask for.

Brutal images flashed behind Elle's eyes. Her parents were dead. Her home burned. A murdering, brutal relation was chasing after her.

It was enough that Elle wanted to close her eyes and

forget about it all. To climb up onto the bed beside Erik and Mary, pull them to her and sink into a dark sleep. But forgetting was not an option. Sleeping was also not.

After the meal, they cleaned up their bowls and cups, and the two young ones did fall asleep. Glenna returned to weaving her basket. But Elle could not be still. She had to move. She had to continue on. Sitting here would do no one any good. Aye, she'd sent the messenger ahead, but *she* needed to get ahead, too. To explain the urgency. To tell them her parents had been killed.

"Have ye a horse?" she asked softly of Glenna, glancing at Erik to make certain he was asleep.

"A horse, my lady?" Glenna glanced up from her weaving, her brow furrowed.

"Aye." Elle swallowed hard. "I need to get to Dunstaffnage. I sent a lad, but in case he doesna make it, I need to warn Laird MacDougall."

"Why do ye not ask Barra to go when he returns? He'll not be long now."

Elle shook her head. "Nay. I've already sent one messenger ahead. I need to go myself. Besides, I need Barra to stay behind and protect Erik and Mary." She thrust her chin toward the sleeping children. "They canna bear the long journey. 'Tis too dangerous for them. Please, if ye dinna have a horse, then point me toward a croft where I might find one."

Glenna set down her basket carefully. She studied Elle for a long moment before finally relenting. "We've a horse, but I dinna think Barra will be happy about ye going alone."

"Please, I beg ye. The longer I wait, the longer it will be before help comes. The devastation... What happened…" Elle couldn't put to words the torment she felt in her soul. "My parents are…gone."

Glenna let out a shuddering breath, but nodded slowly. "I

understand, my lady. Ye need not explain. I will tell Barra 'twas necessary."

Elle breathed a sigh of relieve. She thrust the bag of bannocks onto the table. "Take these. They are from the castle and should keep the children fed a little bit. I will bring back your husband's horse." She looked regrettably at the children. They would be angry that she was leaving, but it would be easier and less painful to do so while they slept. "Please tell them I will return. That they need not fear."

"Ye have my word, my lady, they will be safe. I'll look after them as though they were my own. Barra wasna lying about your parents. They helped us escape from Ireland and set us up here with the croft."

"They were good people," Elle choked out.

Glenna looked stricken, taking in her past tense use of their existence. *Were.* "Aye, my lady, they were." She shook her head and placed a comforting hand on Elle's shoulder. "Rest assured, they'll be safe until ye return. We've a nook under the house where we hide when raiders come. If the Vikings make it this far, I'll hide them there."

Elle gripped Glenna's hand, squeezing, and blinking back tears. "Thank ye. I will see that ye are greatly rewarded for your kindness."

*S*cottish Highlands
*1207*

THUNDER STRUCK SO VIOLENTLY THAT THE WALLS OF Dunstaffnage Castle seemed to shake and the floor vibrated beneath the feet of every person in the great hall. Several prominent members of the clan stood around the perimeter of the vast chamber, their eyes not locking on anything in particular. They sipped their whisky and avoided speaking of the reason for their gathering, though 'twas on the tip of every man's tongue.

"'Tis raining something fierce outside, my laird," a passing servant said, pouring him yet another cup of dark, strong ale.

Laird Beiste MacDougall still wasn't used to being addressed as *laird,* a title that had belonged to his father until just that morning.

He grunted, holding his cup to his lips and draining the contents in one long swallow. An hour or more had passed since his tongue had gone numb from drink. He planned to continue drowning his sorrow in ale until he fell asleep right there at the table. Beiste stretched his legs out, tapping the bottom of the cup on the wood until it was filled again. His gaze roved from one man to the next, taking in his uncles, cousins. The women huddled closer to the kitchens, probably plotting his future. Aunties and cousins, he was related in some way to all of them, through his mother or his father.

And now it was just him.

His parents were gone.

His siblings were gone.

His wife and child, also gone.

He was all that was left of the MacDougall Clan. The elders would be harping on him soon to take another wife, but he couldn't just yet. Maybe not at all. How could he risk failing another when he'd failed everyone who'd ever counted on him? Aye, he'd not been to blame specifically for the deaths of his siblings—all three had passed just hours after being born. But he was the only survivor and he couldn't help but wonder if he'd somehow ruined the womb for the rest. Why had he survived and they had not? It had made him extra strong on the battlefield. Extra determined to be victorious at all things—after all, there was no one else to succeed him. He was the only chance at his father and mother's line succeeding.

Of course, that contradicted his desires not to find himself attached to a new woman, to beget another child— yet, it was the only way to fulfill his duty to his family.

The loss of his first wife and child…he blamed himself entirely for their deaths. When his wife insisted on going with him on campaign, he should have said nay. Should have told her to remain at home. But he'd been weak with desire, with what he was certain was love. He'd allowed it and she'd become pregnant. She hid that fact from him, not wanting to distract him with the news or be sent back to the castle. By the time he'd figured it out, it was too late. Her horse spooked, tossing her to the ground. Her labor pains came swiftly after and there'd been nothing he could do about it. His own selfishness had caused the death of his beloved. Of his poor bairn son who had squealed in his arms for only a few breaths before passing on.

He'd vowed from that moment on that he'd not be taking another wife. Not with the shroud of death that cloaked him. Anyone close to him died and, so, he kept everyone he cared about at arm's length.

Duty to his clan first. Other than the begetting of an heir…

Fierce pounding sounded through his skull and he rubbed at his temples. But he realized the incessant banging wasn't blood pummeling the inside of his skull, but the main doors to the keep.

"Who in bloody hell is knocking?" he growled, slamming his cup down. Anyone worth their weight would simply enter.

A tingle crept over the back of his neck. Was it Death himself?

"I will go and see," Gunnar, his Master of the Gate, and second-in-command said. He bowed to Beiste and walked toward the door.

"Nay. I'll go." Beiste pushed himself out of the chair, his feet feeling heavy.

Gunnar nodded, waiting.

Despite the numbness of his tongue, Beiste's head was surprisingly clear. Then he took a step forward, wobbling only slightly. Not enough for anyone to take notice, save for himself. Mayhap his head was not as clear as he thought.

No matter. With a hand on the sword at his hip, he trudged beneath the archway into the main vestibule, aware that every eye in the great hall had finally found its mark. *Him.*

He ignored them all. Ignored the questions in their gazes.

The stone vestibule was dimly lit. A single torch about ten feet away cast shadows on the great wooden door that vibrated before him.

The banging continued until he wrenched open the door.

Standing in the dark, in the pouring rain of the bailey was a woman, a cloak covering her from head to toe. Only the tip of her pink, pointed nose and the rosy glisten of her lips shone in the torchlight from the vestibule. Her figure was slight, her shoulders trembling. She was soaked through to the bone.

What in bloody hell? Beiste swiped a hand over his face, frowning fiercely. Perhaps his quest for numbness had affected his eyes. He was seeing things now. Mayhap it was best if Gunnar did deal with this. 'Twas a certainty now that the ale he'd imbibed had the ability to make him feel less drunk than he was, or at least to make him think he was less intoxicated.

For certes the sopping wet lass was a figment of his tormented mind.

Beiste closed the door and turned around to go upstairs. He needed to sleep. 'Twas one thing to get drunk from grief and pass out in his cup at the trestle table, another thing entirely to find himself talking to ghosts.

But the banging returned, pounding through his head with incessant urgency.

Och, bloody hell! Beiste whirled on his feet, a growl on his lips, and prepared to tell his demons to take a hike down a long and winding path.

When he opened the door this time, the woman glared up at him with wide, green eyes that seemed to glow from the torch flames. Intense. So vivid. He fisted his left hand, and gripped the door hard enough with his right, that he feared he'd splinter the wood to keep from reaching out to touch her—if only to make certain she was truly there.

"Are ye real?" he asked, realizing his question was odd and gave away his inebriated state. But all the same, he needed to be certain.

"As real as ye are," she hissed. "Will ye let me in or force me to catch my death?"

Beiste cocked his head. Was this a trick question? "How did ye get past the guards?" He stuck his head out the door, raindrops pelting his skull, to see his men still walked the walls as though they'd not just let a strange woman into the castle.

Her shoulders straightened. "I'm here to speak with the laird. Let me pass."

Beiste crossed his arms over his massive chest, blocking her way in and attempting to put fear into the woman with his sheer size alone. "Ye didna answer the question."

She didn't even seem to notice how much bigger he was. If anything, her glower deepened. "I'll only be answering to the laird."

Beiste bit his tongue. He *was* the laird, but this chit wouldn't know it yet. The storms had been so bad since his father passed that he'd not yet sent out word to their neighbors of his death. Besides, the elders would want to do so, formally inviting all those in their holding to come forward and give their blessing and allegiance to Beiste.

"Do come in," he said gruffly, affecting a sloppy bow meant to mock her sharp tongue. He stepped back, allowing her space to enter.

"Thank ye." She swept past him as though she owned the place, hands in the voluminous skirts lifting the hem away from her feet, head held high. She brought with her a faint scent of fresh rain and earth. Of spring. Beiste raised himself up, trying to take in that she was truly here.

The lass stopped abruptly and turned to face him, brow furrowed, lips pursed in consternation. "Something is not right."

He studied her as she pushed the cloak back, revealing dark hair with hints of red.

"I quite agree," he murmured.

She was really quite beautiful. Enchanting even.

"There is…" Her lips clamped closed. She shook herself, as though trying to shove off whatever reservations she now suddenly had about being inside his fortress. "Bring me to the laird. I must speak to him. 'Tis of the utmost urgency."

Beiste grunted, re-crossing his arms. Who was she that she could order him about? She carried the airs of a lady, but what lady traveled alone in the rain at night?

"Nay." He was curious to see what her reaction would be to him denying her.

Her eyes flashed on him with disdain. He had the feeling she were assessing him, that he was not standing up to whatever magnitude she theoretically measured him against. "I am not asking."

Beiste's eyes widened at the haughty tone that brooked no argument. 'Twas on the tip of his tongue to put the lass in her place but, instead, he decided to give her exactly what she wanted.

"Come," he demanded, stalking toward the stairs.

His father's body still lay abed, where it would remain until the rain ceased and they could put it out to sea on a great pyre as he'd requested. An ancient and worthy burial for a man who'd been as great and fierce as all the ancient kings, including Beiste's own grandfather.

Beiste didn't bother to take a torch with him. He could climb these stairs in the dark and he kind of wanted the haughty wench to trip behind him—as uncharitable as that was. Though to be fair, he didn't want her to get hurt, either. He kept a keen sense on her, so if she did, in fact, trip as he wished, he could quickly catch her, too. He might be a beast at heart, but he wasn't cruel unnecessarily.

Surprisingly, up the three flights of stairs they went and she never once faltered. Not even on the sixteenth stair that had risen in the middle creating an unsettling foothold for anyone who traversed it. Nor on the twenty-seventh where a large chip had been broken from the tip of the step when someone dropped a heavy boulder on it during the construction. That had been some twenty years before when the Norsemen had ruled heavily in the area. Only recently, with his father, they had worked to bring Scotland together as one unified country.

Dunstaffnage was the most well-fortified castle for hundreds of miles around. Mirroring the Norse skills and use of stone to build fortresses that were impenetrable, it featured walls ten feet thick in places, rising high and mightily into the sky.

At the third floor, he nodded to the guard standing outside his father's chamber. The man glanced curiously behind him at the woman he'd let in, but said nothing. Beiste was fully aware how odd it was to bring a stranger to see his father's body. But he didn't care. He wanted to see the shock on her face. For her haughty nature to dissipate.

He opened the door, the scents of illness and death washing over him in a hazy, thick wave. Beiste swallowed, suddenly hating his own plan. His father's soul, freshly gone from his body, would no doubt frown upon him. The lass was about to get a fright and he'd be the one to blame for it.

Behind Beiste, the lass gasped. He turned in time to see her cover her mouth with the back of her hand, her eyes widening and meeting his. Her entire body shuddered, and he doubted it was from the cold, wet garments.

"He is gone," she murmured. Tears glistened in her accusing eyes. "Ye didna tell me."

Beiste swallowed and cleared his throat, feeling it constrict with emotion at seeing his great father brought down. "This morning."

Her trembling increased. Fingers shaking against her throat. "I am too late."

"If ye wished to speak with him, then aye." Beiste swallowed back the bitterness he felt. There were so many things he had yet unsaid. Why had he not gone in his father's place? Demanded to go? He could have saved him…

The lass dropped to the floor at his feet, her hands covering her face, shoulders shaking. She hunched into a tiny wet ball, stricken. Beiste jolted. Shocked, and uncertain what do to.

"Are ye crying?" Beiste asked, suddenly uncomfortable. He regretted the sound of disdain in his tone. He'd never had to comfort a woman before, as his wife had been quite cold. Now he found himself completely at a loss. An intense need to escape made his hands and feet tingle.

Who was she and why should she be sobbing at his father's death? Beiste had been present for most of the days his father opened the castle up to the clansmen and women and he'd never once seen her before. At least. Not that he could remember.

She glanced up at him, tears streaming over her creamy cheeks. Green eyes glistened in the torchlight. "Ye have the disposition of a beast."

He shrugged. "I am aptly named."

She wiped at the tears with her wet cloak, not succeeding in soaking them up, but rather spreading the wetness more over her skin. "I am lost. We are lost." Her words were soft but unmistakable.

"I am not lost," he said.

She glanced up at him sharply, venom in her gaze. "Not ye, ye fool!" Rage filled her tone, so much so he took a step back before realizing what he'd done.

No one had ever spoken to him that way before, well, save for his ma and da when he'd done something incredibly dangerous or stupid as a child. But he was not a child now. He was laird. "I'll caution ye to guard your tongue." His voice was brusque, but seemed to do little to deter her temper.

Fisted hands punched at the floor. "And who are ye to caution me?"

Beiste was about to tell her he was the laird's son. Though he was, it was time for him to claim his title. To let the raging wench know just who she dared speak to in such a way. "I am Laird MacDougall."

The lass blanched. Mouth agape, eyes wide. Slowly, she pushed back up to her feet, standing at her full height, and met his gaze. When she spoke it was only slightly louder than a whisper. "I must apologize for my…temper."

Beiste ignored her, instead more intent to find out just who this guest was. "Who are ye and what business did ye have with my father?"

"I am Elle Cam'béal."

The name was familiar to him and he racked his fuzzy brain trying to dredge up the reason. "Am I to know ye?"

She frowned, glancing toward the still body on the bed. Beiste looked, too. The familiar ruggedness of his father's face was showing, his body still as full and bulky as he'd been in life. He could have been sleeping. The ravages of death had yet to set in. The deep gash in his chest was bandaged, covered with a plaid blanket. His death had been swift. Less than twenty-four hours from his return from the road.

They'd yet to find out who had attacked him as the men he'd ridden with had all died in the skirmish.

"I had hoped ye might. But it would seem he never mentioned my family."

Beiste reined in his impatience. "And they are?"

"The Cam'béals. We live...not far from here at Castle Gloom."

Beiste grunted. "The Irish warlord. I know of him. He's a vassal of my fath—of mine."

"Aye." She chewed her lip and he watched her suppress a shudder. "He was."

"Married to a Norsewoman."

She nodded. "Aye, my mother. Our family's lands were given to us." Her voice was low and soft. More tears gathering in her eyes. "By your father. He was our protector."

"He protected all in his realm."

She shook her head. "There was more...my father...he saved your father's life once, in a battle. So, Laird MacDougall swore an oath to protect us for all time."

"What are ye doing here?"

"I came because... I..." She swallowed, the column of her throat constricting. "How did he die?"

"An attack on the road."

She gasped and took a step back. "Recently?"

"Aye. Yesterday he left the castle with his men, only to return a short time later. His men dead. A mortal wound to his chest. He died this morning."

"I am so sorry."

"'Tis not your fault."

She shook her head. "That is the thing...'tis my fault. I summoned him." Eyes wide, she jerked her gaze away from the bed and met Beiste's eyes. "Ye're all in danger. They are coming."

Beiste saw red for a moment. The source of his pain

standing right before him, ominously foretelling of more tragedy. "Who is coming?"

"My mother's family. Vikings."

"What?" Beiste moved quickly, grabbing her by the arm and dragging her within inches of him so he could stare into her eyes. The muscle of her arm tightened, well formed, she was still slight, fitting in his palm. He could snap her in two.

She flinched, but kept her gaze on him when anyone else might have closed their eyes to ward off his ire.

"Explain," he demanded.

"They attacked several days ago. Killed my father. They stoned my mother in the bailey, naming her a traitor. They set our castle on fire. I hid my brother from them, but it is only a matter of time before he is found. They will kill me. They will kill ye."

Beiste gritted his teeth, working every ounce of self-control not to throttle the lass. His father had been killed by Vikings. Summoned into a fray by this slip of a lass.

"His death is on *your* head."

"I didna know they would kill him…"

"Aye, ye did. For did they not kill your own?"

Her shoulders slumped. "I thought he'd bring a legion of men. I warned him of the attack."

"Ye thought wrong," Beiste growled. Even as he said it, he wondered why his father had not brought more men. Why he'd ride off without even explaining what was happening to Beiste.

Anger raged inside him. He couldn't talk to her anymore. Couldn't look at her. Feared he might lose his temper, incited more by the ale swimming in his veins.

His grip still tight around her arm, he dragged her from the room and up a level where his own bedchamber was. He flung open the door to the chamber attached to his own and thrust her inside.

"What are ye doing?" she asked.

Beiste fought to catch his ragged breath. He felt as though a fire had been lit in his lungs, his throat. "Taking ye prisoner." He glowered down at her, fresh anger gutting him. This was for her own safety. From *him*. "Dinna attempt to escape."

"Wait," she called, arms outstretched as he slammed the door closed, stabbing the key into the lock and twisting.

She banged against the door, the pounding sharp and hurting his head. "Please! Ye must help my people. My brother, Erik, he must be rescued!"

Beiste ignored her wails as he retreated, charging down the stairs to the great hall. There was no time to think about her pleas. Nor could Beiste think about his father's oath, his promise, his vow to protect the Cam'béals for saving his life, not when his own had been forfeit in an attempt to help. A promise wasn't linked to blood was it? Wouldn't be passed down to him to honor would it? Och, but Beiste knew it was. He'd have to honor it, simply because his father would have wanted him to.

"Gunnar," Beiste called.

His second-in-command stood at attention near the bottom of the stairs.

"Vikings are coming. They are who killed my father."

"How?"

"We've had a visitor. She told me."

Gunnar raised a brow, perhaps questioning the ale he'd drunk. "A woman."

"Aye."

But then the man let out a resigned sigh. "A guard came in to give ye this. She carried it with her. They found it on her horse." Gunnar held out a weighty claymore, the iron hilt carved with thistles and roses, and embedded with a large emerald at the very top. "Thought ye'd recognize it."

"That is my father's sword. It went missing when I was a lad."

"Indeed. And what was she doing with it?"

"I dinna know. But I'll found out." Beiste gripped the hilt of the sword that had been passed down to his father by his father before him, the great Norse king, Somerled, who'd come to conquer the land.

"There was this, too." Gunnar handed him the baldric strap. On one side was the MacDougall crest, and on the other the Cam'béal.

A show of fealty? Beiste shook his head in confusion.

He glanced toward the archway, where just a trip up the stairs would take him to the room housing the mysterious beauty with his family's sword and the answers to his father's death.

What had his father gotten into? Why hadn't he told Beiste about his oath of protection to the Cam'béal Clan?

"Prepare the men on the wall for a siege. Send out riders to warn the villagers. The Norsemen are not merciful. They are brutal. Everyone must take shelter if it is not too late already."

## 3

*E*lle shivered in her heavy, wet clothes. The room she'd been tossed into was dank and dark. Around her ankles, a chilly draft swirled. If it weren't summer, she might have thought icicles were forming.

A sliver of light shone near the wall, and she approached on unsteady legs, her body achy, tired and her mind utterly exhausted. She slid her feet carefully over the stone floor, unfamiliar with where furniture might be or a discarded item that could hinder her path.

All hope seemed lost now.

Against the stone, her fingers fell across a thick, fur covering and she tugged it aside to see outside. A blast of cold air hit her face, a spray of water as the rain hit the stones to splash back against her. The storm still raged, angry, violent.

Men ran about the darkened bailey, their bodies shifting and swerving in lurching shadows. Bulky beings dressed in wool. Wet hair plastered to foreheads. When lightning flashed over the sky, she caught brief glimpses of them.

Fierce and hard, these men were. Miniature versions of their new laird.

The vast heath beyond the castle was dark and bleak. With every strike of lightning specters on the moors, trees, wildlife, maybe the Vikings, came to life in minute flashes.

The choppy waters of the sea crashed wildly against the shore, competing with the thunder for sound. If she had Erik here with her, she might try to steal a ship. Bribe someone to man it for her, take them both far away from here. Perhaps Ireland, to her father's family.

A crash below brought her attention back to the bailey. Someone had dropped something. A basket full of stones, maybe? What were they doing below? Suddenly shifting into such quick motion. Preparing for battle? Had he heeded her warning? Did he believe her?

Did that mean he would come and set her free?

Or would he give her away when the Vikings came?

The warrior in question thundered into the center of the bailey, barking orders, hoisting heavy barrels up the wall toward the wooden walk below the ramparts. Oil? Stones? Weapons? She watched him work, mesmerized by his strength and agility. Fluid moves that stretched the linen of his shirt across broad shoulders. The new laird was a force to be reckoned with.

Elle's shivering was incessant now. Water dripped from every inch of her, creating a puddle on the floorboards beneath her feet. Teeth clicking, fingers trembling, knees knocking. Elle dropped the flap and worked with her numb fingers to untie her cloak, heavy with rain. The weight of its removal made her sigh as her shoulders lifted. But her gown, too, was soaked through and cold. Gooseflesh pebbled her cold skin. Her fingers ached from having clenched them for so long.

She shuffled against the wall, making out the outline of

hearth. Kneeling before it, she felt inside, touching rough wood, then lifted against to the mantel, searching out the flint rock. It took her more times than she cared to count to get a flicker of any spark to light the damp kindling, but at last, when her fingers felt raw and she thought she'd collapse from exhaustion and chill, the flames caught.

Elle sank to the floor in front of the slowing growing fire, removing her boots and hose, wiggling her wrinkled toes toward the flames and wincing at the way the heat ached on her frozen limbs.

When she could feel her feet again, she disrobed down to her chemise and laid out her gown and cloak to dry. The room lit enough for her to see. Stone walls, a narrow window, wide enough for, perhaps, herself to fit through, but not a larger man. She spied a four-poster bed with a plain brown curtain tied at the posts. A thick, brown blanket covered the mattress The floor was bare of any rugs, but was scrubbed clean of dust. A single chair and small table were situated near the hearth and beside the door was a narrow wardrobe not quite as tall as herself. There was no person-ality to the room, no personal flare or even a hint of what clan the room belonged to. She could have been anywhere in Scotland, if she'd not known exactly where she was.

The wardrobe revealed several more blankets, and she could have collapsed with relief that warmth was soon to be in her grasp. She pulled a blanket from the wardrobe and wrapped it around her shoulders, sinking back to the floor before the hearth.

She sat like that for an hour or more. Time seemed to stand still, the flames mesmerizing, the heat taking away her chill and the pain of having lost her family, of having to leave her brother behind. For a moment, she was numb to the disappointment of having found the laird gone, and his surly son in his place.

But then it all came crashing back into her. The defeat of the days' past and present.

For that's what had happened wasn't it? She'd lost. There was no telling what would happen to Erik and Mary, what could have happened since she'd left them in the care of Glenna and Barra. It had taken Elle nearly five days to reach Dunstaffnage. Two days more than it should have, because of the storm, and because the old nag she'd been riding had to walk more than run.

A soft knock sounded at the door. She knew instantly that it wasn't Laird MacDougall. He would have pounded. Nay, he would have simply burst inside. There was nothing soft about the warrior laird.

"Who is it?" she called, almost laughing bitterly because it didn't matter *who* it was. The door was locked from the outside. She wasn't going anywhere. She wasn't going to open it with a friendly greeting. The knock was a courtesy only.

Through the door a woman's voice sounded. "His laird-ship requests ye come down to the great hall for your supper."

Elle's stomach growled, but she refused to give it attention. She'd suck the water from her cloak before she accepted a meal from a man who'd rather lock her up than help her. "I'm not hungry," she lied.

There was a pause, and then, "My lady, he *quite* insists."

Elle could practically hear the wringing of the woman's hands on the other side of the door. Did she fear she'd be tossed out on her ear if Elle didn't come down? It was almost enough to agree. *Almost.* But not quite.

"Nay." Elle used her most commanding voice, the one she used on the hounds at home when they had hold of one her slippers, or the way she would have commanded a child to put down a sharp instrument. Let the woman tell the laird that *she* was *quite* insistent.

There was no reply, only the soft retreat of shoes on the wooden corridor floor.

Elle's chin fell to her knees and she stared into the flames. Her chemise was nearly dry, her hair no longer dripping rivulets.

As soon as her other things were dry, she was going to figure out how to escape, because one thing was for certain— she was *not* going to be a prisoner to Beiste MacDougall.

BEISTE STARED DARKLY AT THE DOOR OPPOSITE HIS LARGE OAK chair. He sat in the chair, in the dark of his chamber, brooding. No candles lit. No hearth fire.

That door—that *blasted* door—behind it, was a woman he wasn't quite clear what to make of. Was she his enemy? An ally?

Not an ally, for she was the reason his father was dead.

But not an enemy, either.

After working with his men to prepare for the impending attack of Vikings, he'd gone for a rigorous swim in the sea to clear his mind of drink and grief, and to rid his body of sweat. To awaken his muscles. To prepare.

Having ordered his men to take shifts on watch, he'd decided to get some rest before dawn made itself known, but here he was, sitting in this chair, staring at that door, instead of sleeping upon the massive bed against the far wall.

Sleep would not have come to him even if he tried. He should go back downstairs, relieve Gunnar from watch, and take his shift.

Beside him, the emerald on his father's great sword

winked from the flash of lightning that sliced through the bearskin covering over his window.

A storm like this would last for days. The heavens mourning for the loss of his father as much as Beiste was.

How had Elle Cam'béal come into possession of his father's sword? Had she stolen it? Or was there some unfathomable way in which it could have been a gift?

*Why* had his father rushed off to fight a battle that had nothing to do with him?

Some of the questions that ran rampant in his mind could only be answered by his father. Others, he might be able to find the answers to from the feminine body that lay beyond this door.

Beiste twisted his neck, cracking the tension out. He gripped the wooden arms of his chair, feeling the curves of the wood bite into his fingertips, and he pushed himself to stand. He stalked toward the door, his boots echoing in the silent chamber. He was prepared to push through and demand the answers he sought. Demand she tell him everything or suffer the consequences. What consequences he wasn't certain. He'd not have her beaten. And already the woman had refused to eat.

Had refused his hospitably. Preferred to starve.

There'd been no feast in the great hall when he'd told the housekeeper to go and fetch her. Only a plate set for the lady as it had long been past the hour of supper and in her condition he was certain she was in need of sustenance. His men were fortifying the walls, and it had occurred to him, that though he begrudged Elle her position, hospitality still held its place among those of their stations. A lady should be offered a meal; she'd clearly traveled a long way and would be hungry.

It had also occurred to him that she might still be cold,

wet. He should have told the housekeeper to find the woman some dry clothes. Extra blankets. To light a fire for her.

Beiste gritted his teeth.

Wet. Cold. In the dark. In a strange place. Behind a locked door.

He'd not treated her well. Even for a prisoner. She was a lady, and deserved to be given treatment according to her station.

He reached for the handle. Another flash of white criss-crossing the room, shining on the iron hinge.

Beiste pulled his hand back, reminding himself that he was attempting to make things right by her. He should not simply surge through.

Rather than doing so, he lightly tapped on the wood.

No answer.

He tapped again, a little harder this time.

Still, no answer.

The lass could be ignoring him. Or something could be wrong. How was he to know if he didn't check? Beiste put his fingers back to the iron handle and lifted. The door made a creaking sound as it edged open, and he peered inside, toward the low embers of the hearth.

She'd lit her own fire? Nay, the housekeeper must have come in to do it, seeing that he'd been neglectful.

Beiste scanned the room, half expecting to see her fuming in the chair by the hearth as he had been just now. But it was empty, save for some billowing fabrics.

His gaze was drawn toward the bed. From somewhere in the middle of the vast mattress came soft snores.

She was asleep. Not ignoring him. Not harmed. Asleep.

He should go.

But his feet moved forward instead of backward, and he took in her tiny shape in the center of the bed, piled high with blankets, the curtains partially closed except for where he was certain she could view the door and the window.

Fiery curls fanned out over her pillow, catching the light from the sliver of moon shining through a gap in the fur and the window.

The room was warm from the fire. Near the hearth, he made out the shapes of her clothes, left to dry. The heaps of fabric on the chairs, that's what they were, her clothes.

Again, his gaze roved back to her. She was not wearing anything beneath those blankets.

Heat filled his blood, but he forced himself to quell the sudden burn. Just because a woman was not wearing any clothes did not mean she was there for the taking. Beiste was not a lecher.

But this woman… this one so filled with spirit, so enshrouded in secrets and unanswered questions, she interested him. Still, he could not simply take her. Bedding a woman, an innocent woman at that, went against his moral code. For certes, if he happened across a willing wench—a widow preferably—he was not one to turn her away, there could be much to benefit from mutual pleasure. But an innocent woman… A young woman in his care—even if she was his prisoner—was not to be bedded.

Beiste stared at her a moment longer, thinking she looked angelic lying there. So vulnerable. An overwhelming urge to curl her up in his arms and vow to protect her filled him. Was it the drink he'd had too much of that day? An ethereal pulse from his deceased father, urging him to honor the vow? A warrior's honor? A laird's duty?

How was it possible for her to look that way, for him to feel this way, when she'd brought about so much death? When she represented the downfall of life as he'd known it?

The reminder of why she was here, what she represented, was enough to push his steps backward toward the door.

Once again in his own room, he shut the door, leaned his head against the cool wood.

Exhaustion made his bones heavy. Grief made his mind so. Apprehension over the impending Viking invasion warred with his body's need for sleep.

The walls were fortified, messengers sent out to his villagers and crofters. There was nothing more to do tonight but wait. While he should get some sleep, he knew it would not come for him. He'd relieve Gunnar, stand watch until his eyes fell heavy.

In the morning, he'd reevaluate what to do with the chit. Ask her the questions that needed asking.

ELLE'S EYES HAD BURST OPEN AT THE SOUND OF FOOTFALLS behind her. Boots. A man's boots.

He'd come from the connecting door, not the one that led to the corridor.

Beiste had been in her chamber.

Alone.

What had he been doing here?

She'd kept her breathing even, shallow. Didn't want him to know that she'd woken.

Would he… She'd swallowed hard, her hands fisting against her nude thighs. Her chemise had ridden up around her waist as she slept. Only the blankets served as a protection from his probing eyes.

*Probing.* She felt so exposed. Vulnerable. Knowing his eyes had been on her as she slept there, so indecent, made her body flush with some foreign sensation. Made her want to roll over to see his face.

What had he wanted?

She'd waited, breathing slow, letting every few exhalations sound like a soft snore. Her heartbeat kicked up a notch and it was an active hardship to keep her inhales from hitching. Oh, she'd wanted to turn over. To demand he leave. Or, wicked lass, demand he stay.

Her back had been to him. She couldn't see what he'd been doing, or wearing. Was he also in a state of disarray? His plaid wrapped around his hips, but no shirt? His shirt, but no plaid? Oh, to have seen and read his expression, to understand what his intent was.

Fear clawed at her at the same time his scent washed over her. Male, earthy, a hint of spice. She'd closed her eyes, as if doing so would be enough to will him away. But it only conjured images in her mind of what he was doing. Despite his beastly manner, his constant frown, she'd have been blind not to notice how intensely handsome he was. Dark, rugged. She wanted to smooth her hands over the sharp angles of his jaw.

He was rough with her because of grief. Because he blamed her for what happened. That didn't make it acceptable, but at least she could understand him better.

His footsteps had faltered behind her. And then he retreated back through the door, the soft click of the hinge going into place.

Elle had waited for the sound of the lock clicking, but there was none. Only a very soft thud against the wood. A fist? A head?

She rolled over, as quietly as she could, tugging her chemise back over her hips and down her thighs, feeling the instant warmth of heated fabric covering chilled skin. Her eyes remained riveted on the door, waiting for him to change his mind and come back. To wake her and demand whatever it was he'd wanted.

When he did, she'd demand her own things. Her needs. Her brother's safety.

But he did not come back, at least not while she was awake, nor did he wake her as she drifted in and out of sleep.

Beiste MacDougall did haunt her dreams though. And in her dreams, he crawled into bed behind her, his large heated body pulling her softly against him, warming her all the way to her bones. Sinking against her, his scent powerfully heady. The stubble of his chin glided over the skin of her naked shoulder as he whispered into her ear, *"For a beast, I am aptly named. And by no lass shall I be tamed, save for the one whose stolen my soul, the only one to make me whole."*

## 4

*E*lle woke with the dawn, the inky pink of the sky shining through that small sliver between the wall and the fur lining. A sheepskin, soft and curled at the edges from age. She shifted the fur aside, peering out into the dim light of morning. The men still walked on the walls, their backs rigid. A fire was lit in a brazier in the center of the bailey, and several servants hurried to and fro.

Though she'd woken with the dawn, it appeared many had been awake for hours—if they'd ever gone to sleep.

The storm had receded some, but ominous clouds shifted in the distance, touching the pink lights of dawn and threatening to unleash themselves at their own pace.

Elle moved quickly to don her gown, working at the laces at the front of her bodice. The wool was tight from having been so thoroughly soaked, the laces stiff. She tugged on her hose and laced up her boots, then threaded her fingers through her hair, working to get the knots out of her long curls. It proved a painful pursuit, and so she gave up, wishing she'd a comb, or at the very least a ribbon to tie her unruly mane into something manageable.

Her stomach gurgled with fierce irritation, and bile rose in her throat, burning the back of her tongue. She choked on it, gagging slightly and wishing that she'd not refused dinner the night before. At the very least, that she'd accepted a crust of bread. This day would not be any easier.

"Strength," she whispered to herself, and turned to face the closed connecting door of the laird's chamber.

After her dreams, after the odd sensations that had coursed through her when he entered her chamber the night before, she wasn't certain how to proceed. How to feel... What to say. Could she look at him with the same hostility when she'd imagined him holding her? When her mind had conjured up words of... She didn't dare give voice to what those words had meant. *For a beast, I am aptly named. And by no lass shall I be tamed, save for the one whose stolen my soul, the only one to make me whole.*

Elle wasn't one to normally give credence to such things, but... the dream had been so real. The words so potent. Even now her face heated, her skin prickled.

She shook herself. None of that. He was her unwelcome jailer. She needed to make him see the right way of it.

Forward another step she went. Determined now.

When he'd shut the door the night before, she'd not heard the click of the lock. And that meant she could open it. She could venture inside and stand beside his bed and demand he go looking for her brother. Demand he not keep her locked up here. Demand he honor his father's oath of safekeeping. Beiste MacDougall clearly did not understand what was at stake.

Elle took three marching steps toward the door before she stopped, her belly flopping, and not from hunger this time, but from nerves.

What if he was not asleep? What if he had risen and was getting dressed—but stopped, nude, when she opened the door? What if he was eating? Or stoking his fire? Or with someone else? A lover…

Elle shuddered.

The man had given no signs that he would be kind to her. That he would not lash out if she burst through his door. The only signs he'd given, quite blatantly, were that he was a surly drunkard, that he wanted her to feel pain at his father's passing and that he blamed her for the old laird's death.

Except, he had come into her room quietly the night before. As though he were checking on her. Looking to see if she was asleep. Warm. Maybe to apologize.

If he'd come for a more nefarious purpose, then he would have attempted it, wouldn't he?

Och, but she didn't know. She didn't *know* him at all.

Elle wrung her hands in front of herself.

"Strength," she said again, a little louder this time.

For Erik. For her mother and father. For her clan. For all those who counted on her. Wee Mary. Mary's brother… Oh, saints, had he been among the dead?

She forced herself to take several more steps, coming nearly to the door when three taps sounded from the other side.

Elle stumbled back, completely losing not only her train of thought, but her courage. Knocks? As though someone was expecting her to come to the door? To be ready…

"Aye?" she said, hating the tremor in her voice. Her eyes roved over the wood to the handle, waiting to see it lift.

"Are ye decent, my lady?" 'Twas the MacDougall, his voice muffled and gruff.

Elle straightened her shoulders. Folded her hands demurely at her waist. "Aye."

"May I enter?"

He was asking her permission? When she was his prisoner and he'd so boldly entered the night before?

Elle huffed with both confusion and frustration. She was ready to offer him a rebuke, but instead, said, "'Tis your castle."

The door opened, and there he was, filling the expanse. He'd cleaned, shaved, the fragrance of whatever lather he used, spicy, earthy, lightly scenting the air. Tendrils of golden, glossy hair hung loose around his tanned, chiseled face. Eyes the color of the storm clouds outside met hers.

"Ye're dressed," he said.

She narrowed her eyes. So, he had taken note of her disrobed state the night before. Or perhaps he was innocently surprised to see that she'd already risen. Elle doubted that, this man exuded everything but innocence.

"As are ye." She took in the crisp, clean *leine* that stretched over his broad shoulders and muscular chest and arms. His plaid, muted reds, greens and blue. Pleated to perfection, a thick leather belt slung casually at his hips with sporran that centered in the front. She stared a little too long at the sporran, feeling her face heat with embarrassment when he cleared his throat. She'd only been looking at the etchings in the leather, but she didn't need to explain that to him. Likely the beast would find some way to bring her further mortification. So, instead, she snapped her gaze back to his and said haughtily, "Did ye think I'd allow ye entrance otherwise?"

He grunted, a crooked grin touching his non-frowning mouth. Without the frowns and glowers of the night before, she couldn't help but notice just how handsome he was. "Ye did not come down to sup last night."

"I wasna hungry."

"Come down to breakfast now."

He started to turn around. A man unused to being denied. But who was he to place demands on her?

Elle crossed her arms defiantly. "Nay."

Beiste turned back around slowly, narrowed his dark

eyes, brows furrowing. If she'd not already given herself a talking to before he knocked, she might have backed down. In fact, her belly was begging for her to back down, but she could not accept his demands. She'd have to bribe a maid to bring her crust of bread, something, anything, later. Her point needed to be made—she was not a prisoner. Nor was she going to do as he said, simply because he said it.

"Ye'd rather starve?" His voice was lowered, nearly a growl. A warning.

Elle swallowed past the hunger. "I didna say that."

"Then what?"

"I want ye to help me. I want ye to help my brother. I want ye to set me free. I did not come here to be your prisoner, but to seek aid."

He shook his head. "We remain here until the Vikings come."

"But Erik…" She bit down hard on her cheek. He'd said *we*. He'd not denied her. Only the time. All she could do was pray that Glenna and Barra were keeping her brother hidden. That the Vikings had not laid waste to their croft when they passed over the land. If they had indeed passed over the land. "What if they never come? What if they found my brother and are holding him for ransom? What if they've killed him already?"

Beiste took a step closer to her. He was so tall, nearly a foot taller than her. She had to lean back to look up at him, else stare at his boots.

"What do the Vikings want?" he asked.

Elle shrugged. "What they always want. Land. Gold."

"They have that if they stormed your castle as ye say."

She felt the hardness of his stare as he regarded her. He knew she was hiding something. "They do. But they will want the heirs to the land…gone."

"Why? Who are ye to them? Why would they not simply lay claim?"

Elle sighed. She could give him some partial truth. "We are blood to the men who attacked. My mother's kin. They seek…revenge."

Again, that infuriating grunt. "Come break your fast. Eat. Regain your strength."

Elle fisted her hands at her side, hoping the tightness would bolster her nerves. "I want your word."

Beiste shook his head. "I'm not prepared at this time. I must await your kin's attack. I canna give ye my word yet, lass."

"I am a lady."

Beiste bared his teeth at her, and for a moment, she imagined what it would be like to meet him on the field of battle. She'd likely die of apoplexy before he even raised his sword. "I canna give it, *my lady*."

"Ye're a coward," she ground out, knowing it was the furthest thing from the truth. But she'd spoken in anger, before she could pull the words back.

His face darkened and he took a menacing step forward, crowding into her space, taking her breath. "Might I remind ye that ye brought the enemy to my lands, *my lady*. That your enemy has killed my father. That I have people here to protect. Dinna dare to call me a coward, when I am remaining here to protect what is *mine* from what is *yours*."

Elle wanted to sink inside herself. She was the coward. She should have simply taken precautions, taken the time to bring Erik here. But even as she said it, she knew it would have been impossible. As it was, she'd struggled to get here herself, and she was half-starved, exhausted, and weak. Even after a night of sleep, she felt faint with exhaustion.

She, Erik and Mary would still be out there, possibly

captured by the Vikings. As much as she hated to admit it, Beiste MacDougall was her only hope.

At this rate, all she could do was wait for Bjork and his warriors to attack Dunstaffnage. To regain her strength and pray that this man, this beast, could protect her and what was his, so that he could help her reclaim what was hers.

Elle straightened, holding her head as high as she could, her neck feeling as though it might snap. Her fingernails bit into her palms and she worked hard to keep her tears at bay.

"Forgive me," she choked out. "I spoke in anger. In frustration, for I, too, want only to protect what is mine. To protect the future of both our clans. There was no warning that Bjork was coming. That he'd... kill my parents. Your father." Her throat tightened, cutting off any other words she might have spoken.

The laird's face softened slightly, the crease between his brows no longer so indented, his flat mouth no longer so severe.

"It seems that perhaps we have something in common then," he said.

"A mutual need to protect?"

At that, he grunted. That infuriating sound that seemed synonymous with all his answers. "Loyalty, my lady. Your father was loyal to mine and vice versa. Mayhap, there is hope that we will also share a mutual relationship."

Elle narrowed her eyes. Whenever a man talked to her of mutual relationships, loyalty, it often came saddled with marriage. She stiffened. She did not want to get married. Marriage was the furthest thing from her mind. "That remains to be seen." Her voice was colder than she intended, but she could not allow him to believe there was anything more between them than what was already there.

The fierceness returned. "I'll have cook send up your meal if ye willna join me in the great hall to break your fast."

"'Tis not necessary."

"Ye will not eat? Ye'd starve? How will ye be any help to your clan if ye're a bag of bones?"

"How can I be of any help to my clan as your prisoner?"

Beiste crossed his arms over his chest, glowering down at her. She mirrored his stance, but his eyes riveted to her breasts where they were pushed together just above her crossed arms. Elle let out a frustrated sound, and then shoved her hands to her side.

"Ye really are a beast," she hissed.

"How so?" He was goading her now, a mirthful twinkle in his eye.

"Ye know how. For… staring." She glanced toward the window, wishing she could go pull back the fur and leap through it.

"Staring? I am nothing if not observant."

She jerked her gaze back to his. "What ye were observing was not for ye to… observe."

"And what was *it* for then?"

The *it* they were both referring to was actually a pair, her breasts. How absurd that she was even having this conversation with him. These thoughts. Heat filled her cheeks.

"Ye're incorrigible," she muttered.

He cocked his head to the side, his arms still crossed, that twinkle remaining in his eyes, a little crook to his mouth giving him the barest hint of a smile. Dark eyes searched her face, then roved lower, taking in the entire length of her body at an agonizingly slow pace. By the time he reached her toes, Elle thought her face might burst into flames.

She stomped her foot and let out a little growl, starting to sound a bit like him. "How dare ye?"

Beiste chuckled. "Ye thought me to be staring before when I only glanced at the *its* ye so proudly showed off. Just, now, aye, that was staring. A keen observation." He stepped closer, and she refused to back away, warmth flooding her. "And it was… pleasing."

"Get out," she ground out, mortification, and an unwanted heat warring within her. The feel of his arms around her from her dream the night before, returned. *For a beast, I am aptly named. And by no lass shall I be tamed, save for the one whose stolen my soul, the only one to make me whole.*

"The prisoner deigns to order the captor."

"I do. Now get out." Her tone was breathless, her strength leaving her.

Beiste gave her a mocking bow. He was good at that. Then he backed toward their shared chamber door, sending her an exaggerated wink before closing it behind him. She listened for the sound of the lock but heard none. Even still, she wouldn't go through that door, if only to find him sprawled on his bed waiting for her. That look… That roving stare had heated her from head to toe, and it could only mean one thing. His talk of loyalty and all that… He wanted her. Or he wanted her to think he wanted her. A game?

The man was exasperating.

And she wasn't going to fall for it. Not for all the heated glances in the world.

Beiste MacDougall could go to the devil.

## 5

*I*n the great hall, two places had been set at the trestle table on the dais as Beiste had instructed. Men filled the other long tables, gobbling up their porridge efficiently as none of them knew just when the Vikings would attack.

The second place at the dais, beside his own, had been for Elle. Mrs. Lach his housekeeper glanced behind him, frowning.

"She's not coming. Send her breakfast up."

The housekeeper moved quickly to remove the place setting, signaling a servant to clear it. The serving lass made eyes at him, offering her sympathies and no doubt something else. Beiste ignored it.

Now that he was laird, he could not dally with those who worked at the castle. There was something wrong about the measure of power he held over them. He could never be certain if they actually wanted to bed down with him, or if they felt pressured because of who he was. Before he'd been married, before he was laird, those sorts of thoughts had not occurred to him. But since his wife's passing three years ago, he'd not lain with a woman. At first out of mourning, and then out of discipline. He was much more focused, alert, when not bogged down with feelings of desire. Perhaps though, he was more frustrated. Taking a *leman* might be a good idea. She'd know her place was only for pleasure, nothing more.

At that thought, Elle's face flashed in his mind. *She* could never be his mistress.

With a sigh of irritation, he sat down and spooned his porridge. The taste was bland. Not that it was usually anything other, but this morning it tasted especially so. His mind wandered back upstairs, to the chamber connected with his own, to the stubborn chit who occupied it.

Thunder cracked once more outside, rumbling throughout the walls. The storm had given them a brief reprieve that morning and now fully revived itself.

He set down his spoon. Listened. The thunder sounded different this time. His blood ran cold. The same tingle he felt with every impending battle skated up his spine.

Beiste was certain the rumbles were masking the din of riders. The Vikings, whom normally would attack from the sea, were instead traveling over the heath from Castle Gloom. They'd travel by horse. The thunder of hundreds of horses. Aye. 'Twas them, for this rumble did not cease. There was no pause between claps.

They'd come.

Beiste and his men had been waiting what felt like days, but in reality was not more than one since the lass had come the day before. His eyes met Gunnar's. The man had also heard the rumbles.

"They have come," Beiste announced.

"Aye," came the reply of most of his men.

Beiste stood, slammed his hands on the table and stared out at his men, meeting their eyes one by one. "Ye fought valiantly for my father. Now fight for me. For all MacDougalls. Prepare for battle."

Beiste rushed out to the bailey in time to hear his men shouting over the high, thick walls of the castle, built from the rock of a mountain and overlooking the sea and heath beyond.

"We will not be sieged this day," Beiste bellowed. "Fire your arrows. Dinna let them over our walls. Fortify the gate!"

Men rushed all around him, rain wetting their hair and causing it to stick to their faces, soaking into the thick wool of their plaids.

Beiste let out a battle cry filled with equal amounts of rage, sorrow and frustration. He felt like a man walking blind into a battle, fighting a war he had no knowledge of. An enemy he'd never met and knew not their motivation. The realization was unsettling but did not discourage his determination. He was considered a great warrior and leader and proud of it.

Beiste marched up the wooden stairs to the battlements, looking down at the rough, soaked warriors below. War paint was smeared across their faces and, streaked by the rainwater. Hair braided and knotted. Long beards. There were maybe fifty to seventy of them. Not the hundreds he'd been prepared for. Beiste grinned. These men worked to make their outside appearances look crude and the stuff of night terrors. But he wasn't scared. Nay, already he knew their weakness.

"Give us the woman!" The bellow from beyond the wall was clear, spoken by the tallest of the Vikings.

*The woman.* They wanted Lady Elle Cam'béal.

Like hell he'd heed their demands. Besides, Beiste wasn't in a giving mood today.

"Ye'll not be getting her today. Nor tomorrow. Ye'll have to kill me first," he shouted. "The woman is *mine*."

THE WARRIOR MOVED LIKE A SPECTER.

Flashes of Beiste's muscled body lit in the lightning-streaked sky, glinting off the long, jagged dagger he held in one hand and the wicked sword extending in iron-might from his other.

In one place for a moment and another the next. Ducking, twirling, dodging, leaping, crashing, hacking at the bones of Vikings. His enemies had nowhere to go. No way to save themselves from his assault.

These same enemies who'd attacked her castle days past were no match for Beiste and his skilled warriors.

Elle had been lucky to escape alive.

By either of them.

Her belly knotted into a thousand tiny, impossible twists. Laird MacDougall's declaration still burned in her ears. *Ye'll not be getting her today. Nor tomorrow. Ye'll have to kill me first. The woman is* mine.

What he'd spoken of, loyalty, mutual relationship, the heated looks… She'd been right to assume he meant to keep her. But for what purpose?

She was *his*. A possession, but yet not claimed. What did that mean? His to protect? To imprison? Abuse? Murder? Wed? Or to set free?

Elle prayed it was the former and the latter, but nothing in between.

Her eyes glazed as she watched the battle raging below. A life for a life. Her life for Erik's. She was willing to give it. That was essentially what she'd told MacDougall before. Although she'd not been completely honest. She'd not told

Beiste the reason her own father had been able to gain not simply a trade of one life saved for another but, in fact, protection for his entire family for all the days of his life.

And she wouldn't tell him if she didn't need to. If he set her free, then she was free. If he promised to continue to protect her, then her secrets were her own. But... if he chose to harm her, her family, or keep her in any way that impeded the oath his father had given, she would tell him.

*Oh, Erik... Pray be well.*

Visions of Bjork and his men crashing against the small croft made her head swirl. She prayed the danger had passed them by. That Glenna and Barra were able to hide Mary and Erik, and to hide themselves.

Guilt riddled her at having essentially left them to fend for themselves.

She wished she hadn't had to, but there was no other way! Where was Bjork now? She'd not seen him, though she'd recognized his voice. The same chilling evil that she'd heard when he'd banged through the walls of Castle Gloom.

Bjork, had come seeking revenge for the lands her mother had claimed. But he'd come for another reason, too. Elle recalled it just then, in a hazy flash. A conversation she'd heard her parents whisper urgently months before. Bjork had decided Elle was to marry him. That he would take the lands through her. And Erik... As long as those loyal to her and her family kept Erik's identity safe, then he could remain hidden and unnoticed by her mother's cousin. Forgotten, she hoped, because a male heir would supersede a female any day, not that such things mattered in a siege. But male heirs grew up. Male heirs garnered loyal, fighting men that could exact revenge.

And... Her hands came up to touch her neck, as if that would help her breathe any better. If someone, Glenna, Barra, the lad who'd run her message, any of the crofters who knew of their escape, anyone truly, thought to gain favor with Bjork... Erik would be in mortal danger.

Elle's stomach grumbled and the dizziness that had been threatening to consume her filled her head like a thick, hazy cloud. She swayed on her feet, reaching out to grab hold of something, anything to keep herself from falling.

She shouldn't have refused breakfast. But even she knew that if she'd accepted, there would have been no time to eat before Bjork arrived.

The chamber pulsed in and out of her vision.

Her mind reeled.

Why was this happening to her? A rhetorical question, truly, for she knew the reasons why, she just didn't want to accept them.

One moment, she'd been with her family. Laughing. Loving. Learning. Living.

The sound of that Viking horn, the same sound that now echoed out her window would never leave her. Castle Gloom had not been as heavily fortified as Dunstaffnage. The Cam'béal holding was small, situated between two larger, wealthier castles. If ever raiders were to come, 'twould be the other castles that they would target. But not when the prize was Elle herself.

Bjork was not an honorable or good man. But rather a man steeped in misery. Jealousy. He hated the Scots. The Irish. The English. Hated anyone not fully Norse. And he'd always resented the marriage her mother had made in order to widen their alliances. Hated that her mother had taken the lands in Scotland that Bjork believed should have been his. He thought he should have been sent to conquer the land, to take control of all the Scots. He thought Padrig Cam'béal too weak to see the deed done, not understanding the need for a greater, more unified Scotland.

As she thought more about it, piecing together the tiny

bits she could recall, Elle realized Bjork's appearance could only mean two things: One, her grandfather, King Ederlad had passed away and, two, Bjork had come to make Amma Cam'béal pay. To take over their lands and castle. To murder and maim and punish.

Bjork had been victorious. But he wasn't done yet.

Elle's father had fought. He'd fought so hard. She could still see him crashing to the bailey ground, blood pooling around him. The way Bjork had stood over his body, breathing heavy, excited. The man had not simply killed for self-defense or in the name of battle, but for the pure enjoyment of it. And her mother…

Elle stumbled forward onto her hands and knees. Her vision blurred. The ghosts of the past finding their way in and out of her line of sight. The bed loomed up in her vision and she attempted to crawl forward, to reach for it, and curl up beneath the blankets. She was suddenly so cold.

But the further she went, the further it seemed. When her gown caught on a stray nail in the floorboards, she simply collapsed, curling up in a ball on her side. After a few deeply drawn breaths, she rolled onto her back, briefly seeing the ceiling overhead. Maybe it was best if she sank into the oblivion that threatened. Maybe it was best to join her family.

But, Erik…

Her brother, so much younger, was unable to defend himself. Mother warned them to never tell Bjork who Erik was. And hopefully Glenna had told Erik that Elle was coming back for him. That she'd not abandoned him. Hopefully, he'd listened. Hopefully he'd forgive her if she was never able to return.

Elle's eyes slowly blinked closed and then back open, the room fading in and out.

She startled at seeing a shadowy figure looming over her.

Outside, the battle still raged.

Who was this? Had the Vikings cut through the warriors and made their way into the keep? Was it someone sent by the new laird to finish her off? In her weary state, she'd not even heard him enter.

"Who are ye?" she croaked, squinting trying to get a better view and not succeeding.

"Laird MacDougall." His voice was different from Beiste MacDougall. Deeper, scratchier, more familiar. The *old* Laird MacDougall.

Her vision came slightly back into focus and she could see that it was, indeed, the old laird, long, gray beard and matching brows. He stood tall and strong over her. Whatever wounds he'd succumbed to before his death were gone.

"But ye're dead..." Her lips barely moved as she spoke. Words felt more like a slow exhale. Was *she* dead?

He floated closer. "Be strong, lass. Be strong and I will protect ye."

Elle shook her head, her fingers curling around her middle. She'd gone too long without food. She was halluci- nating. "But ye're gone."

"Nay, I am right here." There was something soothing about his voice now, as though he'd changed his tone to calm her, beckon her. Well, she couldn't let him!

She had to remain forthright, to push this demonical vision from her eyes. "I saw your dead body. Be gone with ye, ghost!"

The vision darkened, coming more into focus. "What is death? Death canna break an oath I made. Ye know the one of which I speak."

The oath. The reason she'd traveled all this way.

"How?" Elle rubbed at her eyes, the vision not leaving. Was this real? Was she already asleep and this a night terror?

"The fairies, the gods, they are not done with me yet."

He sounded so real… Elle pinched her thigh, hard, wincing at the pain. 'Twould appear she was fully awake. Could what he was saying about fairies and gods actually be true? Was she actually considering that? "Did they breathe life back into ye? Can they help my family? Will they?"

"I canna answer to the fate of your parents, lass. But I do know that I have a task to complete and it requires help from ye."

*Her parents.* He did not mention her brother. That must mean that Erik was still alive. "Am I going to die?"

"Not if I can help it."

And how much promise could she believe from a ghost?

"I am here, for a little while longer, to help save my son's soul. To protect ye. And ye can save Erik. But ye have to make a sacrifice of your own."

His son's soul. But which one? Elle opened her mouth to speak but found no words were able to make their way out.

"Do ye know what a *glaistig* is, lass?"

Elle's head rolled from side to side. Her tongue was thick and she found words didn't want to come. She was so sleepy. She needed a nap. Would the figure mind if she simply fell asleep?

"A *glaistig* is a ghost, gifted by the fairies with immortality and tasked with protecting a house, looking after the weak, avenging those who are harmed."

Elle worked around the thickness of her tongue. "Are ye…a…*glaistig*?"

"Nay, lass. The fairies… they want *ye* to be one. To live this life to your fullest and in exchange for their help, that when ye pass from this earth, ye join them, become their green maiden. Protect future clans from their enemies. Protect the weak. Warn them of impending doom."

The old laird's visage faded into nothing, then shimmied back.

Elle blinked, certain she was having some sort of hallucination. She could not have heard correctly. That almost made her laugh. But was she more willing to believe that she'd heard the ghost wrong than to believe she wasn't conversing with a spirit at all? This was utter nonsense.

Lack of food, drink, sleep. The extreme torment of watching her parents be hacked and bludgeoned to death by her mother's own kin had gotten to her. Taken away her ability to manage. Her sanity. She was going mad.

That was it. Why else would she imagine a dead laird coming to her and promising her protection from the grave if only she agreed to be a ghost herself? But not just any ghost, a *glaistig*, one that haunted anyone who lived on these lands for all eternity.

"I canna…" she whispered. "I willna."

She wanted to protect her clan, her brother, but chances were Erik was already dead. Killed by Bjork. And if he wasn't, then she'd already told Beiste MacDougall of his obligation to her family. He would see their clan protected. Find her brother if he was still alive. She had no doubt that he would honor that vow. Well, mostly no doubt. If he were honorable, he would see to the people even though his father's death would have paid the debt in his own eyes since she'd not been fully honest with him.

All that aside, she…she wouldn't be a haunting thing. She couldn't. When the Lord saw fit to take her from this world, then she wanted to rest in eternal peace. Not be doomed to walk the earth forever. With Beiste protecting the Cam'béals, she need not risk her own soul or sanity.

"I need your word, lass. A blood oath. Let me help ye."

The laird's voice was crisp and clear, right next to her. She rolled her head to the side to see that his shadowy figure had taken up residence in a chair, relaxing as though he had all day to wait her out. All eternity, in fact.

"How do I even know if ye're real?" she managed around her thickened tongue.

"I am real."

"The word of a specter in my imagination." She shook her head. "I need more than that."

"Ask me anything. I will know the answer."

"Only because I have made ye up."

"'Haps. 'Haps not."

"How did ye die?"

"I was attacked on the road. By the men outside fighting right now. The verra same who besieged Castle Gloom, the verra reason ye sent for me."

"And the lad I sent to warn ye?"

"Downstairs helping in the kitchens. He wanted to go with me but I told him to remain behind."

"I dinna believe in ghosts." This was a complete lie. Since she was a little girl, she'd often conversed with faint visions. With fairies, with people of her family's past. In the dark, sometimes the beings frightened her. At other times, she felt a serene sense of calm.

Though she tried to push the old laird off as nothing more than a hallucination, part of her believed he was real.

"I want to go home," she said.

"Make the oath and I will see it done."

"Blood," she murmured, closing her eyes, again picturing her parents' slaughter by Bjork. If only she'd been able to gut her nasty relation first. To gain enough strength to take on his entire army on her own. Oh, how she would have loved to watch him bleed.

And now this. This promise, this blood oath. Her soul for the fairies to keep. *Nay, nay, nay.*

Elle looked back up at the ceiling, shaking her head, tears stinging her eyes. This was not a decision she could make.

Who could? Who could rightly say they'd be happy walking the earth for all eternity, never having peace?

"I'm sorry, Erik," she whispered. "I have failed ye. I am weak. I am a coward."

Elle rolled onto her belly, pushing up to her hands and knees, feeling the wood jut into her palms, her kneecaps. She somehow found the strength to stand, albeit with a slight tremble.

"Ah, so ye have agreed." The ghost of MacDougall stood, a smile crinkling his eyes. "I canna hold on to a dagger, so I'll need ye to use your own. Just a tiny prick upon your finger should suffice. Sign your name upon the stone at the window's edge."

Elle shook her head, staring down at her trembling hands.

"Aye. It must be done with a blood oath."

"I will not." Her voice was surprisingly strong. Her spine straight, rigid. She'd made up her mind. Eternal damnation was not the price she wanted to pay. Her mother and father would forgive her.

Erik may not, but he was either already gone or would soon be found by Beiste MacDougall. Either way, his fate was no longer in her hands.

Tingles prickled up and down her arms and legs. Her feet were numb. That same cloudy feeling still filled her skull with a pressure intense enough to make her think of an avalanche of snow crashing down a Highland mountain.

Elle turned to the window, walking slowly toward it, aware that she was giving up. Aware that she was too tired, too filled with grief to keep going.

"The dagger, lass," the ghost said, an urgency in his voice now.

"I have no dagger," she lied, feeling the cold metal of her *sgian dubh* against her forearm and the second one hidden against her ankle inside her boot. She could have pulled her weapon on Beiste earlier when he'd thrust her in this room, but one should only attack when a semblance of victory could be imagined. And right now, in her weakened state, she was fully aware that she'd not be successful in any attack.

"Use the fire poker then."

Elle rolled her eyes at the idea of taking the thick fire poker to her finger or forearm. Any way she went about it with the tool, her blood oath would likely end with her life, for she'd have to stab herself hard with the dull edge of the poker to cut her skin. "I will not make the blood oath." And then she ran toward the window, intent on leaping through the narrow slit, ending it all now. "Forgive me!"

But as soon as she reached the stones, the MacDougall leapt in front of her. Whatever power he'd been able to summon caused a blunt wall of force to shove her backward.

Elle fell on her rear, jarring her entire body up and through her jaw. She was momentarily stunned, unable to figure out what happened until MacDougall loomed once more in front of her—a black shadow, formidable. Any previous doubts of his existence were quickly wiped away.

"Why did ye do that?" Elle's voice was filled with accusation.

"I canna allow ye to take your life. Not if ye're wanting to get out of being the fairies' maiden."

"What?"

"A blood oath is all that's required. If ye choose to end it now, then ye're as good as agreeing."

He wasn't making sense. Elle shook her head.

"So I must remain alive?"

"Well that is your choice." MacDougall tugged at the shadow of a long beard. She had the sense of the stubble not being attached to anything but air and this movement was one he did out of habit.

"But I have no choice! Ye've just said I will be damned whether I throw myself from the window or not."

The ghost shrugged. "I suppose I should have told ye, ye've no choice. But damnation is far from what they offer. The fairies have decided to gift ye with eternity."

She slammed her hands down on the wood floorboards, shouting, "No choice? Then why did ye even ask me? I dinna want their gift!"

"I'm sorry for misleading ye, lass. I'd hoped that if ye said aye, ye'd have thought it was your own doing."

"But ye knew all along I had no choice."

"Sometimes, when there is an appearance of choice, one is more easily able to accept one's fate."

Elle's chest burned with anger. "But I didna choose this."

"I didna choose to be killed by the bastards out there."

"And I didna choose for them to attack my family, either."

"And my family, too, lass. Ye see, life is really only filled with the appearances of choice. The rest is simply our response."

Elle shook her head, her exhaustion evaporating with her righteous indignation. "Nay. I refuse. I refuse to believe I am walking through this life waiting for things to happen to me. I never did so before and I willna do it now. I am a ripple. I am the one who makes a choice and the world must respond to me."

MacDougall chuckled, but rather than it being a jovial sound, it scraped over her nerves. "Ye're a feisty one."

"I am my mother's daughter."

"A Viking, she was. A true warrior."

"Aye, she was." Elle felt her chest fill with pride at who her mother had been. Memorable. Amazing.

"Never met a fiercer woman." He nodded at her. "Ye do remind me of her. I still remember the day I met her. Pulled her from the water myself. Her ship had crashed along our coast."

"And my father? How did ye know him?"

"He was a prisoner of mine."

This part she knew already, but had hoped to learn how her father came to be at the castle. "And yet, ye let him go?"

"He impressed me." The ghost ran his hands through his graying hair.

"How did my father become your prisoner?"

The ghost laughed, ignoring her question. "I loved her. Never stopped. Your father knew that. Perhaps that was why he was able to keep me as his protector." There was something infinitely sad in the specter's tone. "I will leave ye now. I find that pushing ye away from the window has left me drained. But I will be back. We've still a little matter to discuss."

"I will run from ye."

"I expect ye will. Just as long as ye aren't running toward any windows."

Elle shook her head. "I shan't."

"Vow it."

She blew out a deep breath, relieved he'd been able to summon enough magic, or whatever it was, to shove her away from death. She owed this ghost her life. Never again would she allow grief to push her to such extremes. "I vow not to take my own life."

"There is much ye have to live for, Lady Elle Cam'béal."

"Have ye seen the future?" Did he know just what it was she had to live for?

He shrugged. "'Tis more of a sense."

Elle opened her mouth to respond, but suddenly found the room empty. Dark. Her skin no longer prickled. She was utterly alone and left questioning whether or not her vision had been real or the figment of a tormented mind. He had felt very real.

Though her heart thudded and her head pounded, echoing loudly in her skull, outside she could still make out the sounds of battle.

"Pray, Beiste, be safe," she whispered.

As much as she hated to rely on anyone, she knew that she would have to rely on him for at least a little while. He was her only chance of escape. Of saving her family.

Well, besides the ghost…

6

$\mathcal{T}$he enemy spilled over the sides of the wall like ants, faster than Beiste's men could shoot them down, but not quick enough.

His walls would not be breached.

Beiste bellowed the order for flames to be set to those they poured oil over on the ladders and below. Great whooshes of heat surged as bodies ignited, their shouts piercing. Their defense of the walls pushed most of the Vikings back, though a few men did escape the flaming arrows by leaping over the stone.

About a dozen slick figures, dressed in ragged clothes, weapons strapped to every available surface, dropped onto the ramparts.

Beiste had already scaled the stairs to meet them head on, Gunnar at his side. He launched an attack, imagining that each warrior was the one who'd dealt the deathblow to his father and he was simply returning the courtesy. An eye for an eye. A limb for a limb. A life for a life.

No mercy.

Every Norse warrior that made it over was quickly dispatched of and his body tossed back over the wall.

And good riddance.

The leader of the rebel forces did not retreat, however. He looked to be setting up camp just out of reach of the MacDougall arrows—for he'd told his men to shoot and, though they got close, they did not hit their marks. A streak of arrows drew the line between the camp and the castle.

"Ballocks," Beiste growled.

This wouldn't do. To hell with the damned Vikings laying siege. They'd a well in their bailey and food stores were full given the harvest had just been completed. But, Beiste wasn't the waiting type.

He was a man of action. Decision.

And like hell he was going to allow these broody bastards to lay their camp at his doorstep.

Though he felt his father's promise to keep the Cam'béals safe had been met with the giving of his own life, he couldn't bear the thought of leaving them in a lurch when the lass upstairs had said they were in danger. Besides, he ought to know exactly how many of the Norsemen they were dealing with.

Gunnar approached, the blood on his face and forearms rinsing away with the slowing rain. "Shall we send out the elite?"

Beiste grunted. The elite were a select dozen of his warriors, stealthy in their approach and deadly. They were often sent on dangerous missions that required a bit more skill than a simple battle. Beiste had developed the team and trained them himself with his father's approval. They'd been extremely useful with the unrest in the land. "We'll wait until the bastards have settled, not expecting any sort of retaliation from us. Then I'll send them out."

ELIZA KNIGHT

"And what about the lass? Do ye think she brought them?" Gunnar nodded his head toward the men beyond the wall.

Beiste didn't hesitate in his answer. "'Tis for a certainty, but not because she hoped to infiltrate. She was running from them. They followed." He left unsaid the quiet thanks he gave to the heavens for allowing her to gain entry before the enemy had descended. Those bastards would have eaten her alive.

The men gathered the bodies of the fallen Vikings, dragging them into an empty wagon. They would push that wagon through the doors and send the bodies back to their friends. They may have taken lives today, nevertheless Beiste had respect for the dead.

But Bjork…when he got his hands on that bastard, he was going to remove his head and mount it on his wall—the body returned to his homeland.

"Will we be going on to Castle Gloom, my laird, once we've dealt with the ilk beyond?"

Beiste shook himself from the enticing vision of beheading his enemy. "I dinna know. My father would have wanted it. But we need to deal with the men outside. If only we could get one of them alone to question, we'd know how many men were left at Gloom and what their goal is here."

"I think I can manage that. Allow me."

"I dinna doubt your skills, man, but I canna in good conscience send ye out to the enemy alone."

"I willna have to go that far." Gunnar grinned. "There was a man outside the wall. He fell from the ladder they'd built, broke his legs and they left him there to die. He lies there still."

Beiste frowned. If the Vikings were cruel enough to leave injured men to die, why was he bothering to send back the dead bodies? The Vikings didn't even respect their own dead. "Bring him in."

Gunnar rushed off and Beiste turned to stare up at the castle. When he'd been fighting, he'd happened to catch sight of his prisoner as she gazed down on him. Her expression had been too distant to gauge and he found himself ever more curious about her. About his feelings for her. Only a few moments ago he'd been grateful she'd made it to his castle before the Vikings.

However, there was much mystery that remained shrouded around her. The untimely arrival, his father's sword, and the secrets she hinted at. He wanted to talk to her more. There was something about her having his father's sword that spoke to more than a simple oath of a life for a life. She was too damned stubborn for her own good.

Nay, the lass was hiding something and he intended to find out what it was.

The gates were opened and Beiste returned his attention to the task at hand. Gunnar dragged a man through the doors. Despite his broken legs, the Viking kicked and howled something fierce. Beiste marched right over to him and grabbed hold of his throat.

Leaning close to the Viking, he said, "Cease that noise at once. Ye will tell me why ye've come here and anything else I ask. Then we'll have a healer set your legs." Beiste spoke in English instead of Gaelic, hoping the man would understand him, because for a certainty, he knew no Norse tongue.

"Death is a worthier path than giving you anything." The man's English was broken, but understandable.

Beiste growled, grabbing hold of one mangled leg and digging his fingers in until the man sobbed. "The pain can cease if ye will but tell me what I want to know."

Spittle gathered on his lips and he hissed, "Death first."

Beiste locked his eyes, serious, on the man. "Och, I willna be giving ye that, ye slimy bastard. Torment or peace."

The Viking gritted his teeth and spat, the glob landing

close to Beiste but not quite hitting him. Beiste *tsked* and squeezed the whoreson's bones again.

After several agonizing moments in which his eardrums vibrated from the sounds of the man's howls, the imbecile finally blubbered an assent.

"Earl Bjork…he has come to claim what is his."

Finally, the man had given him something. "And that is?"

"The lands. A wife."

"Castle Gloom?"

"Aye. And Dunstaffnage. A path to the sea. He will fight anyone who stands in his way."

Beiste would gladly provide him with a bloody fight. "Who is his intended wife?"

"The lady… his cousin's daughter." The Viking glanced up toward the keep walls as if hoping to catch a glimpse of her.

Beiste ground his teeth and forced himself not to look. He already knew whom the lady was that Bjork had claimed and Beiste wasn't letting her go. "Lady Elle."

"Aye. She must come out or he will burn Gloom to the ground."

*Lying bastard.* Elle had already told him the Vikings had set her castle to flames. Beiste cracked his neck, taking a moment to think. He needed more information, but it was clear the man was going to lose consciousness soon. He had to be careful in his questions to get all the information before it happened. "Where is Bjork now?"

The warrior's eyes rolled back and Beiste slapped his cheek. "Wake up. I asked ye a question."

"Gloom. The castle…"

More lies. Bjork had demanded Elle be handed over to him just before the battle began. "He didna come with ye today?" He gave the man a chance to come clean.

"Nay…" The man swallowed around his thick, dry mouth.

"He tasked us with retrieving her. We followed her when she ran."

The man was lying through his teeth. Their leader had been clearly among them.

Why lie?

Also, there was no mention of Elle's brother, Erik. Not good. That meant they did not fear retaliation from the man. He could have been dead already.

Beiste's mission just got infinitely more interesting. "How many are with ye?"

"Two dozen."

Another lie. "If ye've lied to me, I will see that your legs are re-broken after they are set."

The Viking shuddered and shook his head. "Fifty-seven were here, thirty will have gone back with Bjork. He was here, but I heard him call his guard to go, the others were to remain here until Lady Elle came out. I swear it." The man shivered, his body going into shock, and taking his mind with it as he fell into darkness.

Beiste waved several guards over, issuing orders for the healer to be brought out to see to the wounded and their prisoner. He'd have the man's legs set, but that didn't mean he wouldn't still kill him later.

Of his own men, they'd luckily only sustained a few minor cuts and bruises, no substantial wounds, no deaths.

"Gather the elite. If there are truly only two dozen men left out in the fields, then our men can take them all out."

"Death or imprisonment?" Gunnar asked.

"Let the Norsemen decide their own fates." If they fought to the death, they would die. If they surrendered, they would live.

"Aye, my laird."

Beiste left the bailey, intent on speaking to the lass in his antechamber. But upon reaching the fourth level, he had changed his mind. He didn't mind intimidating his enemies. But for some reason, he thought he might get more out of her if he were to treat her with a touch more kindness— starting with presenting himself clean of all blood, muck and stink.

She'd seemed receptive to his kindness earlier in the day. Hadn't his mother always said something to the effect of catching more flies with honey? Not that he knew why he'd want flies, but it seemed to make sense here. He cleaned himself up and called for a decent meal to be brought up. He'd offer her sustenance, a glass of wine, and he himself would smell of spices instead of battle.

As soon as the tray was brought up, and he was clean, he knocked softly on the connecting door. He didn't expect her to answer and she didn't disappoint. Silence reigned.

Beiste opened the door to see her huddled in the corner on the floor, hugging her knees to her chest. Eyes wide with fear, though the thinness of her lips showed a ferocity she kept at bay. Still, he hated seeing her cornered like an animal.

What had happened since he'd seen her last? She'd been strong, steady, and defiant. Now she looked as though she'd seen a ghost.

Trying for a gentle tone, Beiste said, "I've brought ye some supper."

"I am not hungry," she said, using the same haughty tone she'd spoken to him with earlier. Good to see that though she was on the ground, her spine was still as rigid as ever.

The lass' eyes slid toward the tray he held of cold roasted chicken, fresh baked brown bread and honeyed pears. The hunger that made her eyes widen belied her denial.

"I will set it here." Beiste nodded toward the table, setting the tray down. "If ye decide to eat it, Cook will be pleased that ye tried her fare."

The lass licked her lips, then looked the other way. "I'd rather starve."

Beiste chuckled, recognizing her bluff for what it was. "I've said similar words myself afore."

A frustrated groan left her lips as she whipped her gaze back toward him. "What do ye want? Did ye simply come to torment me?"

"Nay." Beiste locked his hands behind him, taking a relaxed stance and hoping it would help ease her worry. "I came to ask ye a few questions."

"Then be done with it and leave me in peace."

"Would ye truly be in peace?" Beiste shrugged. "Simply an observation, but as a prisoner, I could never be at peace."

A flash of anger sparked across her face. "I knew it was too good to believe ye wouldn't keep me a prisoner."

Beiste stopped his pacing and met her gaze, letting honesty shine through where normally he'd keep himself locked up. "Would ye rather I lie and say ye're my guest?"

The lass swallowed visibly, her lips pursed as she studied him. "Nay," she said quietly.

"Then I will be honest with ye and I hope ye'll return the favor. Until I figure out a few things, ye are under my guard."

The ferocity that had pinched her lips lessened. She watched him keenly as he built up the fire in the hearth.

Still she sat on the floor. That wouldn't do. He walked toward her, held out his hand and waited until she slipped her small palm against his. Her fingers were cold.

"Come warm yourself. Ye've caught a chill."

She allowed him to help her up and then walked to the hearth, warming her hands. Some color returned to her cheeks. "What needs figuring?" she asked.

"The sword." Beiste took in her appearance, to see if she was lying or being honest. He had a certain knack for detecting such.

"What sword?" *Lying.* Her eyes were just a little too wide, her back a little too stiff. She'd stopped rubbing her hands before the flames.

Beiste let out a half-laugh. "Och, my lady. Do ye truly take me for an imbecile? Well, in case ye do, then I will explain. The one that was on your horse. The one that belonged to my father and went missing some years back."

She sniffed and crossed her arms over her chest, closing herself off from him. "'Tis mine." Confusingly enough, that sounded to be the truth.

"Nay," he drawled out. "It was my father's."

The lass shrugged, no longer meeting his eyes. "Perhaps he only had one that looked like mine."

*More lies.*

Beiste scooted out the chair beside the table and sat down. He stretched out his legs and crossed his arms. "I can wait for the truth, lass. I have an infinite amount of patience." In truth, he was pressed for time. If this took much longer, he was actually quite concerned about his *patience...*

As it was, he still needed to send his father off properly. As soon as they'd dealt with the Vikings outside the walls, they would put him out to sea as he deserved.

"I doubt your patience is infinite," she said with a wry smile, turning away from the hearth to face him at the chair. Already she knew him very well. "Ye strike me as more the pummeling type."

Beiste chuckled and stroked his thumb and forefinger over the stubble on his chin. "I have been known to be that way."

Elle turned to face him more. "Why do ye have so much interest in the sword?"

"It was my father's. I want to know how ye came to be in possession of it."

She quirked a brow. "And what will ye give me in return?"

Why did she have to be beautiful? 'Twas as distracting as her personality. He wanted to despise her. To be able to walk away from the chamber and not feel guilty that he'd left her there believing she was a prisoner. But the more time he spent with her, the more he knew that would be a problem. "Ye dinna have any leverage to bargain."

"On the contrary, my laird, I've something ye want verra much." She twirled a tendril of hair, the most fascinating color he'd ever encountered. 'Twas red, yet streaks of black wove their way in and out like a fairy had run her fingers through the long strands.

Beiste pulled his gaze from her hair and focused on the tiny cleft in her cheek. "Ye're clever. Stubborn." What did they call that? A dimple? 'Twas the wrong place to look, because he simply wanted to touch it.

She shrugged dainty shoulders. "I am my mother's daughter." Then she flashed her gaze at him. "A Viking."

Why she sought to remind him, he wasn't certain. Maybe to see his reaction. To elicit one. Needless to say, he was running out of time. "What do ye want in exchange for the information?"

She squared her shoulders, sensing that his patience was beginning to wear thin. "I want ye to give me your oath."

Beiste narrowed his eyes. "In regards to?"

Her chin came up, jutting out in defiance. "My brother. Erik."

Beiste could toy with her, but the flicker in her eyes only told him that she was terrified about her brother's safety. And from what he'd already learned, Bjork could potentially be holding her brother hostage, if he wasn't already dead.

"All right, I promise to bring him back." *Dead or alive.*

Her shoulders visibly sagged with relief. Saints, but he wanted to reach out and pull her against him, to whisper that all would be well. And where did such sentiment come from?

Why did he have such strong, and unwelcome feelings when it came to the lass?

"My thanks, my laird. He was seeking refuge with a crofter and his wife—Glenna and Barra. A short distance from the castle. Beyond the Burn of Sorrows. When ye bring him back, I will tell ye about the sword."

Beiste slapped his knees in frustration, growling, "Nay, nay, nay. Ye simply said my oath. Tell me now."

Her hands flew to her hips, and from the fierceness in her glare, he expected her to stomp her foot.

"I did say your oath, but an oath has to be met. Ye've merely uttered words. Ye must prove to be true to your word."

"Words..." He wanted to throw his hands in the air. "My word, my oath, is my bond. I would rather run myself through than go back on any vow I have made."

"Words that must be put into action." She started to take a step forward, and teetered a moment, remaining still. "I will gladly surrender my life in order to gain my brother's safety. Take it, if ye must."

What in bloody hell? Did she truly believe he was capable of killing for no reason? That he would take her life in exchange for saving her brother? "And if I dinna want to take it?"

"That is your choice, but I would die for him. I want ye to understand that. To understand the importance of his safe return."

Beiste let out a slow breath. The room suddenly felt very tight and sticky. "Ye're a brave lass."

She walked toward him on unsteady legs, tiny boots peeking from beneath the hem of her dirty, torn gown. Beiste took her in, the paleness of her skin, the way her hands trembled. Her cheeks looked more hollow then when she'd first arrived.

"When was the last time ye ate?" he asked.

"I dinna know."

"Eat. Drink. Rest." He stood from the chair and reached out his hand to her. The time for arguing was over. When she was stronger, rested, fed, then they could pick up where they left off.

She stared at his hand, her pallor fading more if possible. Beiste caught her just as she stumbled forward. She was light in his arms, warm, her curves pressed against him. He sucked in a breath, feeling every inch of her keenly. Plush breasts pushed against his chest. Slim fingers reaching around his neck. Long legs fitted to his.

Her breath was soft, slow against the nape of his neck, sending a thrill to race along his spine.

This was what it would be like to embrace her. To pull her against him and kiss her until they were both breathless, desperate for more.

*Mo chreach*, but he couldn't think like that. Blood rushed to his groin, his body responding to the feel of hers. He gritted his teeth against his need. Saints, what was it about her?

'Twas only that he'd not been with a woman recently. That was all he was willing to admit as he stared into her eyes, watching the way her lashes fluttered and then widened at the contact of their bodies pressed firmly together.

Their hearts pounded against each other, breaths heavy for a fraction of a moment more, before she broke his gaze and pushed gently at his shoulders.

"I'm fine," she said, breathless. "Lack of sustenance."

"I'd never dare think ye a lass in distress."

She laughed softly.

Beiste guided her to the chair, reluctantly letting her go. He cleared his throat, forcing himself to gain some composure and repeated himself. "Eat. Drink. Rest. I will go to

Castle Gloom. I will bring Erik back and then ye will tell me about the sword."

She leaned back in the chair and he poured her a cup of watered wine, holding it to her lips. The lass drank greedily, draining the cup.

Beiste frowned down at the food. 'Twas obvious she was starving. "Do ye need me to feed ye?"

"Would ye?" she asked, her eyes teasing. The corner of her lips lifted as though she wished to laugh but did not quite have the energy for it.

"I would." God help him, what was happening? Feed her? He'd never fed another person in his life, but he realized, watching her, memorizing the enticing curve of her lips, that he would indeed, if she asked. "If ye required it." What in bloody…? The lass had turned him into a sap within half an hour…

"I can manage." She sat up a little straighter, grabbing hold of a hunk of chicken and shoving it ravenously into her mouth. She barely chewed before swallowing and then grabbed another piece. "This is good," she murmured around another mouthful. "Please give my compliments to your cook."

"I will." He watched her with interest, never having seen a woman eat with such enthusiasm and vigor before. Not that he would have, as he'd not come across many starving before. He took good care of his people, made sure that they'd all eaten before he filled his own plate.

"Ye're not as beastly as ye would have me believe." She glanced up at him, her brow raised. "Ye know?"

Beiste grunted. "And ye're not as much of a stubborn, spoiled brat as I would have thought."

She shrugged as if she'd heard that before and went back to shoveling food into her mouth, speaking around mouthfuls. "My father thought highly of yours. And of ye."

"I regret that I didna know him well." And he meant that honestly.

"Not as a man, nay." She slurped some wine, then reached for a napkin to wipe her hands and face.

"What do ye mean by that? Not as a man?"

"Ye knew him as a lad. He was…" Her gaze shifted away from him and she chewed her lip before continuing. "… Waylaid here at Dunstaffnage for a number of years." She tore at a hunk of bread. "Ye might have been about ten when he left."

"What is your father's name?"

"Padrig."

Beiste searched his memory, thinking back to when he was a boy and all the men who'd been here, wondering if that's why the name Cam'béal sounded so familiar. There was one man, but it couldn't have been her father. The man was called simply, Irish. He'd been a fine warrior and imprisoned at the castle, let out to help with training or when the castle was attacked. But always put away at night. 'Twas a strange arrangement and the man didn't seem bothered by it at all.

But this Irishman couldn't be her father. A prisoner. Her father was a lord, having been given lands and a castle by his own father. He'd not have done such a great thing for a prisoner, even if the prisoner had saved his life. He would have simply given him his freedom and nothing more.

"Please go," she pleaded. "Tell my brother he is the new Irish. He will know what it means and he will go with ye willingly."

Beiste nodded, feeling the blood pool from his face down to his feet.

## 7

*E*lle sat back in the wooden chair, her belly full and her mind a little clearer. But her hands were trembling, once more.

Emotions ran rampant through her. First the meeting with the ghost and then with Beiste MacDougall…it was all too much. Ultimatums, her future foretold.

Nay, not her future—her *eternal life.*

Since she was a wee lass, she'd prayed for her soul, sitting alongside her mother and father. Praying. Praying that she'd not be damned. Asking forgiveness for tricking her maid into thinking she'd already had a bath or her governess into believing she'd eaten every last bit of slimy porridge. She'd confessed to running through the freshly cleaned, newly herb-rushed, great hall with muddy boots and she'd been forgiven. Absolved.

So, what had she done to deserve this gift as the ghost had put it?

Elle ran tired hands over her face and rubbed at her eyes. She didn't want to think about her eternal life anymore.

Didn't want to believe that anything that had happened in the last week was real. Or that her future, the position of her people, the safety of her brother, rested in the hands of a man she wasn't certain she could trust.

Beiste… Why was he being so kind to her? He'd locked her in this chamber. Taken her prisoner and, yet, he no longer locked the door. He'd said he'd feed her if she needed him to. *Feed her*. Prisoners were lucky to receive food, let alone have it fed to them by their captor.

Trust. 'Twas obvious he wasn't so willing to trust her outright, either.

But despite both of their reluctance… There was a tension that crackled the room when they were in it together. A sentiment she'd never experienced before. And she didn't know how to feel about that. The way her body had come alive when he'd caught her in his arms. Pressed so tightly to him, every contour of hard muscle was evident.

And his eyes… They matched the storm outside. Shadows seemed to clear from them the harder he gazed into her own. What was it about this warrior? About his touch, his gaze, his low, thick brogue, that pulled her from a near faint into complete and utter awareness?

Elle liked and despised it all at the same time. *Wanted* the tingling sensations, and the flutter in her belly, yet, wished it to all go away, too. The man confused her. Her own reactions confused her.

Lord help her, but even her own reactions to him were… unfathomable. She'd complimented him. Hadn't been able to take her eyes off of him, admiring his figure, his face… Couldn't help but find herself wondering what went on behind his brooding façade. And why should she care? She shouldn't. But still…she'd wanted to be the one to wipe the scowl from his face. To massage whatever pain he felt away.

Aye, her family had been massacred. And so had his father. They both ached, in mourning, and missing their loved ones.

Keeping her captive was completely unnecessary. She was no threat to him. Though she understood how her showing up on the night of his father's death could be interpreted as an odd coincidence. How Beiste could construe her missive as being the death knell.

As she often did with people, Elle tried to put herself in Beiste's position. To understand him better. To figure out a way to get through to him.

She could have whipped out her dagger that first night, and demanded he set her free. Demand that he see reason. That he wade through his grief and see, truly see, that she was here for his help. But she supposed he knew that now.

If she wanted, all she had to do was open the door that led into his chamber and set herself free. Even appeal to one of the servants for aid in her escape.

But she couldn't, because doing so would be letting go of the help he'd now promised for Erik.

Unfortunately for her, Elle needed the grumpy laird. Needed the strength of his army to defeat her enemies. *His* enemies.

They had shared enemies. Didn't he realize that made them allies? That's what their parents had been. Beiste knew that and still he resisted.

And the sword...if he made good on his promise of finding her brother, she would have to tell him the truth behind the sword. A truth that would shatter his trust even more. A truth he might very well deny. Elle had to be prepared, no matter the outcome.

She flattened her shaking hands to the table, staring at her whitened fingertips pressed into the wood.

"Stop shaking," she demanded of herself. "Ye will be strong. For Erik. For your clan."

A shout from the bailey pulled her from her mental struggle and she walked slowly forward, pulling back the fur to see a half-dozen MacDougall men ride through the gates toward the Viking camp.

~

THE MEN OF THE ELITE HAD DISPATCHED THE VIKINGS WHO'D set up camp beyond the wall and now it was time to bury his father.

Beiste stared down at the large, imposing figure of his sire laid out in state.

At his nod, he, Gunnar and several of his father's closest advisors lifted up the carefully crafted litter, setting the weight of their deceased laird onto their shoulders.

Once they reached the stairs, they shifted the weight onto Beiste and Gunnar, winding slowly, carefully down the stone steps.

Pipers' music floated up to them, the mournful wailing notes threading through Beiste's bones.

Once outside, they carried the laird to the center of the bailey, whereby allowing the clan time to line up in procession to the banks of the sea.

Beiste paused here, feeling a tug inside himself. He glanced up at the castle, spying the fur pulled back from the chamber that housed his *guest*.

Elle stared back at him.

She should be down here. The lass had lost her father, mourned his own.

"Gunnar, please retrieve Lady Elle."

Gunnar nodded, leaving the litter to run back inside. Several moments later, he returned with Elle, fear in her eyes, but the color having returned to her face.

"Ye will join the procession." Beiste motioned her forward. "Stand beside me."

Elle positioned herself beside him without argument, and he felt her slight tremble. She glanced up at him.

"Ye've nothing to fear, lass," he whispered.

Beiste signaled the men to continue. They marched forward, following the pipers through the gate and making their way toward the crashing sea.

At his order the day before, a great funeral pyre had been assembled. A boat had been filled with kindling, rushes and herbs, and a woven bed of wild flowers awaited the settling of the litter overtop it.

Wrapped in his plaid, his hands folded over his heart, Beiste's father still looked only as if he were sleeping.

They settled the litter on the bed of flowers, and the men each grabbed hold of the sides of the boat and heaved it over the bank toward the water. Cold sea sprayed up at them as the waves crashed, washing chilly over their boots. They pushed until the water reached their knees and the boat floated on its own.

It was time to let go, but Beiste found he didn't want to. He couldn't.

He wasn't ready to say goodbye.

Elle remained behind on the beach. He glanced back at her, seeing the tears streaking down her cheeks.

She mourned with him. Perhaps mourning her own parents who she'd not been able to say goodbye to. That cut deep at his heart. The lass had run away after seeing them cut down, in order to save her brother and in hopes of saving her clan.

She'd run to him.

Beiste nodded and gave one final shove to his father's pyre. The water lapped at the hull and sucked the boat further out to the sea.

Back on the beach, the pipers played and Beiste's best archer waited his signal to fire a blazing arrow at the kindling.

Beiste sighed heavily, returning to the shore. He stood beside Elle, feeling her sag a little against him. Without thinking, he reached for her hand, sliding her fingers over his palm, threading them with his own, anchoring him. A rush of calm filled him. Her touch. Her standing beside him.

Beiste was a warrior. He was supposed to offer protection. And yet, with her hand in his, he had the sudden sensation of being protected by *her*. Comforted.

He gave a signal and the archer let his arrow fly, igniting the pyre in flashes of orange and red.

The MacDougall priest offered a prayer and murmurs of, "Blessed be," followed.

"He was a good man," Elle whispered, her voice catching.

"Aye," Beiste said. "I'm certain your mother and father were, too."

Elle nodded, squeezing his fingers tight. "I'm sorry."

"Ye need not be."

"I am."

"'Twas not your fault. I know that now. I'm sorry for blaming ye."

"If I were ye, I would have done the same." She smiled up at him. Not the indulgent smile of a woman to a man, nor the forced smile of a captive, but one of a kindred spirit. That small curve to her mouth, it gave him so much more, said all the things unsaid.

And Beiste felt it all the way to his core.

They stared out to sea, the pipers playing, the clan silent, for close to an hour, their hands entwined, until the fiery boat was a blip on the horizon. The way that Beiste wanted to remember it—his father there, just beyond his reach, yet still in sight.

"We should return," he murmured.

Those in attendance nodded, voicing their condolences.

Elle gave a final squeeze and slipped her hand free from his. As she retreated, he had to force himself not to pull her back.

8

*E*lle's fingers still tingled from where they'd clutched so tightly to Beiste's.

Standing beside him on that beach, feeling his strength, his warmth seeping into her bones, she'd felt something like never before. A sense of things being right in the world—and yet they were so utterly wrong.

There they'd stood, their feet sinking into the wet sand, watching a great warrior taken before his time being pushed out to sea.

When Beiste's fingers had slid over hers, seeking, needing, Elle had done the only thing that felt right, she'd clung tight. He'd needed her.

Beiste, the fiercest of warrior's she'd ever met, had needed *her* to steady himself.

Elle stared down at her hand, not sure what to expect. She felt changed. She felt… more alive than she ever had.

In the past week, her entire world had been ripped apart, turned upside down, and everything was still so uncertain. Yet, at that moment, when they'd clung to each other, she'd felt it—that sense of purpose she supposed she'd been searching out her entire life.

Her mind flashed back to the visit from the apparition. How, he'd told her that her fate would be to marry Beiste. How she'd resisted. How she still wanted to resist.

They were strangers. Weren't they?

In most sense of the word, aye, but there was a connection there that she'd not felt with anyone else. An unseen force.

Was that the fairies and their blasted predictions?

How was she to know if it was real?

Maybe she'd have to… touch him again?

Elle shook her head, mumbling, unconsciously of her idiocy. At twenty-one, she was nearing spinsterhood. Her father had been indulgent of her wish not to marry, her wish to find a suitable husband and her excessive list of traits in choosing such a match. Fussy was what her mother had called her. Elle preferred cautiously selective.

But this… a minor touching of hands and she was considering listening to the words of a specter? Well… that was just beyond her own comprehension.

She was acting a fool. Letting a little thing… But she couldn't even finish the thought, because what she'd felt on the beach in the wake of her grief was more than a little thing.

Watching the laird drift off to sea, listening to the music cascade in the wind, sinking inside her soul, providing Beiste with the support and comfort he needed, all of it meant a great deal.

Where were the bodies of her parents buried?

Were they buried at all? Were they still lying where they'd crumpled?

Elle's mother had not often spoken about the customs of her Norse relations. When prompted, her face had always grown dark, as though a thousand ghosts from her past haunted her mercilessly, and Elle had always backed off. So, she didn't know if that meant her parents would still be lying where they'd been so brutally cut down, or if Bjork would have seen the dead properly buried.

And she didn't want to think about that. When she stared out at the burning pyre, she'd imagined that her parents were still on it. That Beiste held her left hand and Erik held her right.

She'd mourned. She'd cried tears for all the lost lives, and she'd held herself strong for Beiste. For Erik.

She'd not let go. "Never."

"Did ye say something?" Beiste still walked beside her as they headed back to the castle.

Their footsteps were hushed whispers, scooting over the sand and then the grass toward the main gate.

The pipers still hummed on, leading the processional back to the keep in tranquility.

She shook her head, glancing at him from her periphery vision. "Nay, nothing. I was…" she swallowed. "I was just taking note that the storms had stopped."

"We are blessed. If not, we'd have had to wait longer to light the pyre."

"A sign he was meant to sail into the heavens today."

"Aye."

They walked in silence a moment more. Elle twisted her hands in front of her. Wanting to escape. To run ahead and away, so she wouldn't have the overwhelming urge to say something else comforting. She found herself lacking in words and searching for anything she could use to make herself useful to him. A bad sign. For, she did not want to grow whatever connection had formed between the two of them. She wouldn't be here long. Nay, she was not going to believe in the ghost's words.

She had one oath to follow and that was the vow she'd given her mother on that fateful day. To protect her brother.

"Will ye sit with me in the great hall, have a drink?"

"A drink? I am not thirsty." Her mouth was parched. But she sensed she needed to get back to her chamber, to the boundary of her confinement. There seemed to be a safety there, from the danger of being close to Beiste. She needed time to sort through her thoughts. She also sensed that when Beiste said drink, he did not mean a simply glass of watered ale or wine, but something heavier.

A drink that required conversation.

Companionship.

"Please?"

Elle swallowed, reeling in her need to run and her desire to stay. "One drink," she heard herself saying.

Beiste nodded and though he didn't smile, the frown around his brow faded.

He led her to the hearth that had been lit to a small blaze, emitting just enough warmth to take away the draft of the castle, but not enough to make them sweat.

Beiste slid his hands over the etchings at the top of the chair backing, fingers delicate, the way she imagined he would touch her—and then quickly shoved that thought aside.

"Sit here." Though a command, it came out sounding more like a request.

Elle nodded and swiping her skirts beneath her, sat down, back ramrod straight. Beiste stayed behind her for a few moments, long enough that she wondered if he'd remain.

Warmth crept over her neck, tickling her jawline and then her cheeks.

He patted the curved top of her chair backing as though he'd made up his mind and then circled around to the front and sat in the chair opposite her.

With him finally seated, Elle was better able to relax, sinking into the cushion and even scooting to lean against the back he'd just touched.

Beiste signaled to a waiting servant. "Wine," he said.

Within moments, a pewter wine goblet was in her hand and rich red wine was poured. Beiste was served next, as though she were the lady of the house.

She did not often drink wine, not because she didn't like the taste of it, but because it was expensive and her clan could not afford such luxuries as a practice. Rich wine like this was only brought about on special occasion.

"What is the occasion?" she asked nervously, swirling the red liquid in the goblet and drawing in the scent.

Beiste cocked his head to the side, studying her. "We toast life."

Elle shifted slightly, thinking of her brother. She chewed her lip and looked toward his boots, unable to meet his yes.

"Ye dinna want to toast life?"

"I but worry over my brother. His life."

Beiste grunted. "Then we toast life and the retrieval of your brother."

Elle raised her glass, taking note of her trembling fingers. She nodded, afraid her voice would come out just as shaky as her hands.

Beiste took his glass to his lips and she followed his lead, allowing the wine to spill over her tongue. It was good. Very good. Good enough that she took a quick second sip, savoring the smoky flavor harboring an essence of blackberry.

"Do ye like it?"

"Aye," she murmured.

"'Tis a MacDougall wine."

"Truly?"

"Aye. We distill our own whisky, but I wanted to make

wine, too."

"Ye participated in the making of it?'

"Aye."

"Where is your vineyard?"

"Beyond the orchard. Would ye care to see it?"

She wanted to, but sitting here sipping wine, and the idea of strolling through vines made her uneasy. Erik was likely suffering and she was enjoying a cup of wine as if nothing mattered.

"Perhaps another time," she said.

"Indulge me."

Elle pressed her lips together, unable to refuse because he was laird and because he had promised to retrieve her brother. Furthermore, she was intensely curious to see what a wine grape looked like for she'd never seen one before. One short trip to his vineyard could hurt nothing. "All right."

Beiste waved over the servant who took their empty goblets, and then he stood heading toward the back of the great hall. He paused, turned back around and approached her, offering his elbow.

What was happening?

She expected him to march and her to follow, but the gentlemanly offer of his elbow? Nay… that was not like him. Unless…

He wanted her to think him a gentleman?

Elle's fingers slide around his upper arm, feeling the muscles tense at her touch, then she glided down, over the crook of his elbow, and finally lay her hand to rest on his forearm.

Servants watched them with curious and cautious eyes as he led her through the kitchens out into the herb garden and the orchard beyond. Through the lines of apple trees, they strolled until they came to rows and rows that comprised the MacDougall vineyard.

Trees were trussed up, so that their long vine-like limbs reached overhead in an arch and thick grapes hung up the sides and overhead. The archway formed a long tunnel that smelled fruity and exotic.

"This is amazing," she murmured, not expecting to have seen this. "I've never seen anything like it."

"The Irish was not the only man to have visited Dunstaffnage. We'd a Frenchman before who set it up when I was a young lad."

Elle let go of his arm and approached a wall of green and deep purple. She slid a fingertip over one thick grape, the skin of the fruit velvet.

"Amazing that these little balls of juice make wine."

Beiste edged closer, reaching for the same plump grape, his fingers grazing hers and sending shivers racing along her spine. He plucked the fruit and held it before her.

"Taste?"

Taste a grape? Instantly her curiosity soared. Not only had she never seen a wine grape, she'd never tasted one other than those fermented in her cup.

Without thinking she opened her mouth. Beiste's eyes widened, and before she could close her mouth, having realized the unspoken invitation to feed her, he slid the velvet globe over her lower lip and against her teeth.

Elle bit into the fruit, tart and sweet juice dripping over her tongue. She closed her eyes, chewing the grape with relish, and letting out a soft moan of pleasure.

When she opened her eyes, Beiste was staring at her with an intensity that sparked a fire in her middle, tingling all over. He popped the other half of her grape into his mouth, chewing slowly. Savoring the fruit as she had.

"Watching ye eat that grape was as though experiencing it for the first time myself."

Elle grinned, feeling slightly nervous. "I fear I may sneak out here and eat up the entire orchard."

"Have another." He plucked a second grape, and once again fed her, eating the other half.

Only this time, he pressed closer, his thumb swiping away a drop of juice from her lip. He brought it to his mouth and licked it.

Elle swallowed hard, realizing that being out here with him, allowing him to feed her, touch her mouth... 'Twas dangerous territory.

Beiste's dark eyes were riveted on her mouth. Heat flamed her cheeks and he stepped closer. Would he... kiss her?

Nay! Kissing was...wrong.

But, oh, how she wanted to know what it would feel like to have his lips on hers... Elle's gaze flicked over his mouth. Wide, lush lips. Lips that looked like they knew just how to kiss a woman.

A good thing, since she had no idea what she was doing.

Heaven help her, he was so handsome. So close.

She'd never kissed a man before and she'd be glad for the distraction. A kiss to make this moment complete.

Especially, since she didn't expect to remain at the castle long. Once Erik was found, they'd return to Castle Gloom and Beiste would remain behind.

Elle shifted forward half a step, her boot tips touching his. She tilted her head up to stare into his eyes, and he lowered slightly, coming within a few inches of her mouth.

Her lips tingled in anticipation. She held her breath. Waiting. Wanting.

"I should not kiss ye," he murmured.

"Why not?" she whispered back.

His fingers slid over her arms, light, then firm as he tugged her closer.

"There are many reasons why I shouldn't." His eyes searched hers, roving her face as though he'd commit it to memory.

"Probably hundreds," she murmured.

"And not one reason why I should."

Elle shook her head.

"Except, lass, I have this overwhelming need. An urge so deep I can feel it down to my toes."

Elle touched his shirt tentatively, her fingers wrapping around the slip of plaid that was tossed over his shoulder. "I feel it, too."

Beiste cupped the side of her face and she leaned into his touch, her gaze locked on his, her breath shallow and quick. "Then I will."

There was scarcely time to close her eyes as his lips descended on hers, brushing tentatively, pushing, melding softly. His tongue swiped over her lips and she gasped, opening enough for him to delve inside to savor her.

He tasted sweet and tangy, like the grapes, but more heady, more potent, like grapes that had been fermented in Beiste's own essence.

Powerful sensations swirled inside and outside. Tingling, heated, wonderful. Elle clung to his shirt for balance, her legs wobbly, toes numb.

Beiste was kissing her. Actually kissing her. In all her daydreams as a lass and then as a woman grown about what it would be like to have a man wrap her up in his arms, this did not even compare. His kiss was the stuff of treasured memories, the pain of a broken heart, the pleasure of being wanted, desired.

His kiss was true perfection.

And it was over all too soon.

Beiste tore his mouth from hers with an effort that made it seem almost as if they'd been sewn as one.

He raked his hands through his golden hair, stared wide-eyed at her. Did he feel it, too? Was this kiss as mesmerizing, earth-shattering, and world-altering for him as it had been for her?

Backing away, he shook his head, put his hands on his hips. He opened his mouth as if to speak and then closed it.

Beiste cleared his throat, stood taller, hands now at his sides. He bowed low, and when he stood he said, "Forgive me," before turning around and stalking through the vines toward the apple trees.

Elle stared, too stunned to respond, at his retreating figure, her fingers to her lips, feeling their swollen, tingly surface.

What just happened?

At last, he disappeared, and she could picture him charging through the kitchens and then the great hall, stomping the floorboards into submission.

Well, she couldn't stay here. She couldn't let him simply kiss her and then stalk away as though she'd done something wrong. He'd asked her for a kiss. It wasn't her that had initiated it.

With renewed vigor, and much irritation, she too charged through the gardens toward the kitchen. The servants eyed her, and she felt thoroughly stripped, as though each one of them could tell she'd been kissing the laird in the vineyard.

A lad that stood by the hearth turning a spit caught her attention. Her mouth fell open, and he nodded at her, murmuring, "My lady."

"Ye're safe…" Elle couldn't believe it. The ghost had not lied. Her messenger was indeed in the kitchens.

She started to tremble, tearing herself from the suddenly overheated kitchens and pushing through to the great hall.

The ghost… The old laird… If this was true, then that meant the other things he'd said were true as well.

As she approached the front doors that led to the bailey, she heard Beiste's voice outside, barking orders to his men. She could have sworn she heard him shout Castle Gloom.

Elle stopped dead in her tracks. Castle Gloom. Could it be? She rushed toward and arrow slit window by the entry door, peering outside.

The men stood at attention, listening intently to their leader and then began to gather more riders. Weapons were strapped on. Horses, already saddled, were brought out into the bailey.

Beiste mounted—nay leaped—onto the back of a beautiful, sleek, black warhorse.

He was going to Castle Gloom. *Now.* She'd not expected him to act so quickly on his promise and, truth be told, she'd almost doubted he would to begin with—even if he'd offered to feed her. Yet, there he was, armed to the teeth and seated atop a mighty animal.

Had the kiss pushed him?

Was it the need to get away from her? The need to see his end of the bargain fulfilled so he could so quickly be rid of her?

Elle eased toward the door, unconsciously tugging it open and stepping onto the stairs that led to the bailey.

Beiste turned to look up at her, not at all surprised to see her standing there, as though he'd sensed her watching.

Would he order someone to take her back inside? Did he trust her to remain here, not locked up, while he was gone?

His gaze locked on hers, filled with an intensity that caused her to remember every slight touch and shiver from the vineyard. Beiste's gaze seemed to mirror her own, and she was embarrassed that he could read her so easily, that he should know how much she'd enjoyed kissing him.

Her face flamed red at having been caught.

She stood tall, brushing away her awkwardness and

nodded to him, mouthing *thank ye*, not only for saving her brother, but for trusting her enough that he didn't demand her immediate return to her chamber.

The man was about to risk his life, and that of his men, for her. For Erik. For the Cam'béals.

How could she have ever called him a coward?

Beiste might have been the bravest and most selfless man she'd ever known.

He gave a slight nod, then raised a hand to her and she returned the gesture, unsure of what to think about it.

Hands held tight to the reins, he urged his horse through the gate, his men following in an orderly procession.

"And so it begins," came a raspy male voice.

Elle startled, sensing before seeing the ghost of the old laird appear beside her.

"What do ye want?" she whispered from the side of her mouth rather rudely and not caring about her tone. "Please, leave me in peace."

He chuckled. "He's always been a good lad, if not a bit rough around the edges. Had a hard time of it, that one."

Elle returned her gaze to the bailey, watching the dust gathering in the wake of Beiste's horse, trying to get a sense if anyone else saw the ghost standing beside her. "How so?"

"Not my place to tell."

She rolled her eyes, resigned to the fact that she'd probably never know what caused the dark shadows creasing beneath the eyes of Beiste MacDougall. "What are ye doing back here?"

"I dinna rightly know, my dear. I am here and I am not. I dinna think I have a choice of when I appear."

She grunted, smirked. "Ye're a response to a choice that was made for ye?"

That made him grin. "Aye. Ye remembered."

"How could I forget?" The portcullis was lowered, the

98

gates closed. Elle went back into the castle, found her way toward the stairs and her chamber, hoping the ghost would stay outside. No such luck, he followed right behind. In her chamber, she stared at the table, wishing there was a heady glass of wine waiting for her, though certain if there had been, all she'd be able to do was think of Beiste's mouth on hers. "Go away. I am making that choice for ye now."

There was a whooshing of cool air over her spine as the ghost swooped in front of her. "That's not verra kind of ye. I want to stay."

"Who said I had to be kind to ye? I dinna *want* ye to stay." She waved her hand at him as if she could simply cut through the mist of his form, cause him to evaporate. "We put ye to rest. Ye sailed out to sea."

"No one decreed ye must be kind, of course. Just thought ye might be. Manners, that sort of thing." The ghost played with his long, vaporous beard. "And my body sailed out to sea, not my spirit."

Elle considered wrenching open the door and demanding she be brought more wine. "I willna shoot the messenger, your lairdship. But ye were the bearer of bad news and so I am obliged by nature to reject ye."

"Still holding a grudge, I see."

"Wouldna ye?" She narrowed her eyes. "Why do ye not go and haunt the one who killed ye?"

He shrugged. "Perhaps I will." His hazy form faded in and out. "Ah, I must be off."

"Where are ye going?" Was he going to listen to her? Go and haunt that Viking bastard? Maybe watch over Beiste while he did it?

"I feel a pull. I think I must go with my son."

And then, just as quickly as he'd appeared, the ghost was once more gone, leaving Elle with more questions than answers.

## 9

One tiny kiss from Elle Cam'béal and an inexperienced kiss at that, and Beiste had been ready to shed his clothes. He rode his mount hard, fast, trying to rid himself of the need he'd felt for her. 'Twas overwhelming.

The lass was unlike any other he'd known. Strong. *Mo chreach* was she strong. And he admired that. To have witnessed her parents' brutal death, and still been able to flee for days on end by herself. To tell him she'd die for her brother, to willingly offer that life up to him. There were some men he knew who'd be wary for doing half of that.

Aye, she'd garnered his respect with her strength, her loyalty.

She'd garnered something else, too, when she'd stood beside him on the beach, tears streaming down her face, and being the pillar he needed in that moment. Sentiments he'd thought would never come to cross his heart. Affection. Need.

'Twas the reason he'd asked her to have a drink with him. The reason he'd shared his passion for grapes. He'd needed to see, if those feelings were real, or simply his overwhelmed heart reaching for the nearest person.

What he'd learned staring at her beneath the arbor was that his sentiments were palpable, and gaining in potency.

And that kiss…

The desire he'd felt for her. The need to wrap her up in his arms and claim her for his own, it had been like a mace to the head.

Beiste wanted her.

Needed her.

And that was why he'd left. Before he decided he didn't need to know about the sword, about the past and the secrets she held.

Beneath him, his mount's muscles rippled with the exertion of their journey. They owned the moors, riding hard over the tall grasses and tamped down roads. Easily climbing the mountains and fording the winding rivers that separated Beiste's lands from Castle Gloom.

Every difficulty they passed he wondered just how Elle had been able to do it alone, and his admiration only grew.

The warriors rode through the evening and, finally, in the dead of night, they were upon the fortress, staring down over the moonlit castle.

All was quiet.

Too quiet.

Not even a torch lit upon the ramparts.

Beiste narrowed his eyes, his skin prickling. What in bloody hell was going on? For a castle that had been besieged by the enemy, the place looked deserted. Abandoned. Not the site of a siege or massacre.

"None of the Vikings escaped their camp?" Beiste asked Gunnar who'd led the elite out into the field to take care of their enemies camped outside his own walls before they'd left.

"None, my laird. And no scouts that we could make out."

If none had escaped, then there was no way the Vikings who'd attacked Dunstaffnage could have gotten word back to Castle Gloom regarding his impending arrival. So what was happening? Was it a trap? Had the Vikings known all along? Perhaps guessed that once he'd defeated the men set upon his own castle that his next move would be Castle Gloom?

Was the lass sent as a lure? Had no massacre ever taken place except for the one that had killed his own father? The unsettling images that played didn't sit well with him. He didn't think that was the case. He didn't know why, and he was probably mad because of it, but Beiste trusted Elle. He dismissed the idea of her being part of a trap. She was too genuine.

"Bloody hell," Beiste growled, contemplating retreat. But he'd not be the man he was, the leader he aspired to be, if he simply left without at least investigating. He whistled for his scouts who nudged their horses toward him. "This could be an ambush. I want you to scout the surrounding area for signs of a trap and report back to me. Do not engage should ye catch sight of any foe, unless they attack ye first."

"Aye, my laird."

The men rode out and Beiste settled into the saddle to wait. He and the warriors that remained with him would not dismount. They'd not take their eyes and ears away from the surrounding area in case his suspicions were correct, which he prayed they weren't.

Not much later, his scouts returned.

"My laird, the place is deserted." Calum, one of the scouts, looked just as confused as Beiste felt. "Not a soul in sight, my laird. Not even a trap set out."

The wind blew ominously through the forest and prickles rose along Beiste's spine. He felt as though he were being watched. A thousand eyes on him, or perhaps only a pair, but it was enough to put him on edge. Even his mount twitched his ears and shuffled from side to side.

"We are not alone," Beiste murmured. Even as the words came out, he sensed an otherworldly presence. Prickles along his neck, his skin chilling. He shook his head. Nay, there had to be a human explanation for what he sensed.

His men nodded, all of them looking cautiously around.

Was it his imagination or was there a mist rolling on the ground around their mounts' hooves that had not been there before? The moon, full and silver lit upon them in the woods.

Beiste withdrew his sword, his men following suit. They moved to form a circle, their warhorses' rears bumping into each other as they gave each other their backs, a form of defense should the enemy present itself from any side.

"Show yourself," Beiste growled to the ever growing shadows.

The wind whistled, rustling the trees that surrounded them. The moon cast shadows everywhere, dark in some places and lighter in others. It was hard to make out where the enemy could be hiding, if at all.

A bird of prey made a piercing noise overhead and then there came a rustling from a bush to his right. Beiste did not wait for his enemy to present himself. Instead, he kicked his horse forward, thrusting his sword toward the shrubs, only to pull back at the very last minute when a young lad's face poked free.

"Please…" the lad begged. "Dinna hurt me."

Beiste recoiled, though he didn't sheathe his sword in case this, too, was part of the trap. "What are ye doing hiding about? How long have ye been there?"

The lad shivered. His clothes were torn. And though Beiste couldn't see in this light if they were dirty, the stench alone was enough to beg the affirmative.

"I…" The lad rubbed at his arms and stepped out from the

bush. At his height and the still soft lines of his features, he couldn't have been more than ten or twelve summers. "I am lost."

"Where do ye come from?"

He shrugged. "I dinna know the way."

"Name your clan," Beiste demanded.

The lad's eyes widened into dark circles, his mouth popping open in fear but no sound coming out.

Beiste gritted his teeth and worked to make himself more pleasant though his business was urgent. "Come now, lad, tell me. I willna hurt ye."

The lad shook his head. "I've no clan."

"Your parents are drifters?"

To this, he shifted his gaze around the large warriors and then nodded, rising up on his tiptoes before settling back down, as one does when given an idea. "They are...they are merchants."

Beiste narrowed his eyes, immediately suspicious. "What do they sell?"

The scamp glanced down at his arms and spoke softly, uncertainly. "Wool...?"

Beiste frowned, examining the lad's torn clothes, his too short breeches and tunic. Not even made of plaid, but a thin brown wool that had seen not simply days of better wear, but years and possibly even decades.

"Failing merchants?" Beiste couldn't help but say.

The lad nodded, once more. His shoulders slumped. His chin fell to his chest as he softly said, "'Haps that is why they left me."

Beiste grunted. Perhaps the urchin could be believed. At the very least, that his family had left him behind. Bastards, leaving the poor lad to starve in the woods or be carried off by a predator. Or worse—taken as a slave by the Vikings. "Did ye happen to see what happened at the castle yonder?"

The lad chewed his lip, but nodded all the same, wringing his hands something fierce.

"Tell me," Beiste encouraged.

"They...came and killed..." His teeth started to chatter. "My parents were there..."

Beiste narrowed his eyes on the poor creature. Perhaps his parents hadn't left him, after all, and they'd been killed in the massacre. Anything was possible.

"Where are the Vikings now?"

The waif shook his head, knees knocking together. "I dinna know. They left early this morn or 'haps it was yestermorn." He swiped at tears leaving pale tracks in the dirt on his face. "I dinna remember."

"Did ye happen to catch which way they went?" Beiste knew his question was a long shot, but it couldn't hurt to ask all the same.

"Aye. They headed toward the mountains."

Toward Dunstaffnage. Or to simply seek refuge in a place he'd be less likely to find them. But not the sea, which meant they were not yet ready to leave Scotland.

Beiste let out a growled curse, which had the child nearly jumping out of his skin. He offered a gruff apology. If the castle was abandoned, its inhabitants either killed, fled or taken hostage, this made Beiste's mission all the more dangerous. He'd need reinforcements. But first, they'd have to carry on to Castle Gloom to see if any clues had been left behind.

"Come with us," he told the lad.

The young one shook his head vehemently. "I canna. I've got to... I've got to find my family. Mary, Glenna and Barra, too."

Beiste stared hard at the boy. Glenna and Barra, were the names Elle had mentioned, the crofters she'd left her brother with.

"Was there a man there named Erik?"

The lad's eyes widened. "Nay, no man."

Beiste frowned. 'Haps Erik had already left or been taken before the lad arrived seeking refuge. "What happened to Glenna and Barra?"

"The Vikings…" The lad swallowed hard. "They set fire to the croft. We ran, and I got separated from them."

"We shall search them out. Come now."

The lad shook his head, a glint of defiance in his eyes that seemed out of place.

Beiste frowned, contemplating whether he should simply scoop up the scamp and tell him to keep his mouth shut or to let him wander the wilderness, possibly being eaten in the process, no doubt starving before he found anyone. Nay. That made his decision quite sound. Human decency, not to mention his position in the land as a leader, dictated he simply could not allow the poor thing to suffer. Even if it hindered their mission.

The child had been brave enough to keep an eye on the enemy to see where they went. He deserved, at least, some protection for the night.

"I didna ask ye, lad."

The gulping sound coming from the lad's throat was loud enough to reach everyone's ears and caused a few snickers amongst the men.

The child stepped forward, his feet bare, no doubt covered in bloody, infected scrapes from walking the woods. He had to be half frozen.

"Where are your shoes?" Beiste shook his head. "Never mind. We'll get ye something to wear." He held out his hand to the lad, helping him up behind him on the horse. With the moon shining on his face, the lad looked somewhat familiar. Perhaps a trick of the light or, mayhap, even all bairns looked the same. "What is your name?"

"Er—John, sir."

"I am Laird MacDougall."

That brought about another round of shivers from the lad, which Beiste ignored. He nodded to his men and they rode down the hill to the castle. The gates were wide open. The specters of the keep welcoming anyone who dared to enter.

The scouts quickly dismounted and made a tour of the grounds and keep, while they waited outside. Soon they returned confirming the castle was, indeed, abandoned. Burned out. All signs of life gone.

Any clues as to the Viking who'd taken hold of the place were left in the ashes of small fires, if there ever were any. They'd left nothing behind, not even a feather from the chickens they'd stolen.

"Eat a meal, get some rest. Come first light, we go back to Dunstaffnage for reinforcements. Together, we will ferret out the enemy in the mountains." Beiste glanced around the eerily empty bailey. "Close the gates. I reclaim this castle in the name of MacDougall."

A vision of his father flashed before his mind's eye.

"For now," Beiste added.

He'd honor his father's legacy and give the castle and lands back to Erik Cam'béal as soon as the man could be found.

## 10

"*M*y lady?" A soft tap sounded at the door.

Elle opened her eyes and stretched wide on the bed. Her entire body was stiff from the past days of traveling, the never-ending hours she'd spent worrying and pacing the chamber. Praying, hoping, begging for Beiste to find her brother.

The door opened and Elle watched from the crack in the curtain she'd pulled around the bed (to ward off any nighttime ghostly visitors) as a short, round, middle-aged woman scampered into the room. Her graying red hair was pulled up in a tight knot on top of her head and she wore a white apron over her MacDougall plaid gown.

"My lady?" The woman spoke softly, kindly. "Are ye awake?"

Elle stretched her arms up over her head, wishing she were not. She then pulled the bed curtains open a ways. "Aye."

The older woman smiled at her. "Good morn. I'm the housekeeper, Mrs. Lach. I've brought your morning meal." She pointed toward the table where a tray of food had been set. "When ye're done breaking your fast, the master left orders that a warm bath be drawn for ye."

Elle blinked. Had she heard correctly? A bath? Most ordinary people, let alone prisoners, were not gifted the luxury of a bath. Or warm water to wash with.

She supposed she wasn't truly a prisoner anymore. Not since he'd not demanded she be locked back up. Not since he kissed her. Not since he held her hand on the beach.

A bath… A luxury.

Another kindness he'd shown her. When would they cease? What did Beiste MacDougall hope to gain by his considerations where she was concerned?

More kisses? More retreats to his garden of grapes?

She closed her eyes a moment, relishing in memories of the way his fingers had slid over her cheek, his thumb brushing her lip. The taste of the grapes, and then the taste of him, the slide of his lips on hers, the way his strong arms wrapped around her, taking the world and all her worries and winging them somewhere far.

And now he'd gone off in search of her brother. She whispered a soft prayer up to the heavens that they were all safe and Erik quickly found.

Elle sat up and pulled the curtain the rest of the way open, immediately struck by the scents of the meal laid out for her. A hunk of pork, freshly baked bread, and was that milk? 'Twas not the typical breakfast she was used to. Nay. At Castle Gloom, and she had presumed everywhere else in the world, breakfast consisted of a bit of bread and watered ale, or sloppy porridge—less a household was lucky enough to find a cook who considered porridge an art form. But this, this was a veritable feast.

"'Tis a fine set up," Elle murmured, swinging her legs over the side of the bed, her mouth watering. Suspicion returned, but she shoved it aside. Besides what lass wouldn't mind a few kisses from Beiste?

The housekeeper beamed. "Aye, my laird wanted to be sure ye were pleased and well fed."

"Why?" Elle couldn't help but ask, her mind immediately going to a suckling pig being fattened up right before the slaughter.

Was that his plan? To knock down her defenses? Nay. He wasn't that cruel. He might have a beastly temper, but he wasn't a monster. She knew that. The way he'd treated her the last few days had been anything but dreadful.

"Ye're our guest," Mrs. Lach said, cocking her head to the side in question. "Come eat now. I'll have the bath and water brought up."

Guest. Beiste had said it himself before. Only words, she'd thought at the time, but evidently, he'd made it clear to his servants that she was in fact a guest. An honored one at that.

"My thanks." The wooden floor was cold against Elle's feet. She hurried to the tapestried rug and then climbed onto the chair, sitting cross-legged to keep her feet from touching.

All her worrisome thoughts disappeared at the sight of the food laid out before her. After starving for days, she had a lot of missed meals to make up for.

The bread had been slathered with butter and apple jam. She took a bite of it, savoring the warmth and sweetness. Then the pork. Then a big gulp of milk. If Beiste MacDougall wanted to feed her like this, she'd gladly take it. Her belly rumbled for more, but she forced herself to eat slowly, else she become ill. While she dined, several servants filtered in and out with a large wooden tub that they lined with linen. Steaming buckets of hot water and *scented* soap soon followed.

Saints, but she felt spoiled. She'd only ever washed with chilled water.

The sweet herbal scent of the soap floated across the room to where she sat, beaming at the luxury of it. At Castle Gloom, they used soaps made from tallow and ash. Nothing sweet smelling, but it got the job done. When Mrs. Lach sprinkled thyme into the steaming water, Elle had to clamp her lips closed from nearly crying out with joy.

Her exuberance at the bath was almost too much. She forced herself to sit still, to finish her meal, and to figure out just what Beiste MacDougall was up to.

Good food. A bath?

She might have thought he was wooing her, save for the fact that he certainly could not be. Could he? He had asked her to have a glass of wine with him, taken her to his gardens and kissed her.

*Nay.* She couldn't believe it.

Besides, she wasn't interested in being wooed. With both of her parents gone, it was her job to raise Erik up to the man he was meant to be. She'd have to run Castle Gloom until he was of age. Attend gatherings of the elders; work with them to keep the clan prospering. The last thing she needed was to worry about a brute like Beiste. Aye, she needed him, at present, to help her. But there, all ties ended. She would return home with Erik and rebuild. Fortify.

Their kiss, it meant nothing—she blocked out the voice in her head that shouted, *liar.* Merely a curiosity fulfilled on both their parts. *Liar liar liar.*

Perhaps, in ten years' time, when Erik was able to be a leader without her guiding hand, she could find—

Och, who was she kidding? By that time, she'd be officially an old maid. A spinster. The elderly sister of the laird. As a lass of twenty-one now, her father had been urging her to consider a husband...

Elle sat back in her chair, swallowing around the lump in her throat. Tears pricked the backs of her eyes and she blinked them away, not wanting anyone to bear witness to her grief.

How she missed her parents, Erik. It'd been over a week now since she'd witnessed their murder and left her brother in the care of crofters, but it felt like the hour before. Every memory was still vivid, painful.

Mrs. Lach swept away Elle's empty trencher and cup and, thankfully, ushered her numbly toward the tub. Elle was stripped of her nightrail and climbed into the steaming water, unable to help the small sigh of pleasure—followed by a wash of guilt.

The bath was glorious, and part of her wanted to sweep her sorrow back into the deep cavern in her chest. But that was impossible. The only reason she was enjoying this bath was because her family had been massacred. It was a sobering thought.

She twirled the herbs that floated on top of the water. Mrs. Lach and Beiste couldn't have known was that this was her *first* bath. At Castle Gloom, she washed plenty, using a basin of frigid water in her chamber every morning. Unless it was warm enough, then she made the trek down to the burn with the other women and they washed in the thawed, churning waters.

But this…this was heavenly.

And her mother, her father, they would have wanted her to enjoy it, wouldn't they? Beiste was out looking for Erik, she was keeping her vow.

The hot water loosened her aching muscles, easing away the tension that had been growing since Bjork first made his appearance.

Elle decided that if she was blessed enough to be given this bath, then she wouldn't sully it with guilt. She leaned back, closing her eyes a moment and forcing herself to bring forth a few happy memories, to keep her family alive in her mind.

The time she'd caught Erik letting all the piglets out of the pen, the end result of all four of them covered in mud chasing the squealing, scampering bolts of pink skin. Riding across the moors with her father, him showing her how to fire an arrow, how to aim so the sun glinted off the tip and not her eyes. Her mother, singing and dancing in the solar when she thought no one was looking. Erik curled up in his favorite chair devouring some new text.

These memories would be with her always. A good life, though short, that she would always treasure.

Using the scented soap, Elle scrubbed her body clean once, then a second time, luxuriating in the sweet smell and the tingly, fresh feeling on her skin. She scrubbed her hair until it squeaked, sliding wet tendrils beneath her nose to breathe in the floral essence. Had her hair *ever* smelled this good?

A few more minutes of soaking in the heat and her memories, fingers tapping the side of the tub. But now, she needed to rise.

Elle stood up, her feet beneath the water still warm while the rest of her swiftly covered in gooseflesh. She spotted the linen left for drying on a chair. Just when she was about to climb from the tub, a swift knock came at the door, followed by a sudden rush of air as it was opened.

Beiste MacDougall filled the entryway.

For several heartbeats, they simply stared at each other. Each of them in shock. Eyes wide. Mouths agape. The sensations that he'd ignited with his kiss pummeled her insides, making her skin tingle.

What was he doing here? Oh, saints! She was naked... Yet she couldn't move. Couldn't breathe. Heat covered every inch of her skin like a soft, enticing blanket. Her nipples pebbled, no longer from cold, but from the heated way his gaze swept over her form, lingering at her breasts, her hips, the place between, and then back to her face.

Desire lit his countenance, dark stormy shadows crossed over his eyes. The muscle in the side of his jaw ticked, and from the way his chest rose with a quick intake of breath and didn't release, she got the feeling he was holding it just as she was.

Finally, Elle reacted, dropping back into the water, sloshing liquid over the side of the tub to the wooden floor. She tucked up her knees to hide her breasts and wrapped her arms around them, glad for the soapy, herbal film on top of the water that obscured mostly anything else. "What are ye doing?" Her voice came out throaty, different, not her own. She shivered. But dignity, honor, propriety won out over the intense desire to let him join her. "Get out!"

"I…um…right!" Beiste backed out and slammed the door shut behind him.

Elle fairly leapt from the still warm water, grabbing the linen that Mrs. Lach had left for her to dry with. Trembling, she scrubbed the water from her skin and wrung out her hair, rushing to don a clean chemise and gown that had been laid out on her bed. She ran a brush through her thick hair, wincing at the pain of the knots. Then she marched to the door, whipping it open. A glower was still on her face and a hand on her hip.

Beiste eyed her slowly, from head to toe, as though she'd not even bothered to put on the gown. Every place his eyes caressed, she felt upon her skin. She became hot, tingly, and her belly flipped in a way that caught her breath. For heaven's sake, she *liked* his perusal. She could tell that he *liked* what he saw.

No man had ever seen her naked. None. With the line of thought she'd had earlier regarding her spinsterhood, she'd been certain no man ever would. And, she'd especially not thought that a man would look at her the way Beiste was looking at her now. Like she was a tasty morsel he'd like to eat. His eyes had grown dark as he met her gaze. Her breath caught. Would he kiss her?

Och, but why did she want him to?

He stepped closer and her heart kicked up a notch. Her lips parted. Waiting. Wanting. His mouth on hers had been about the only right thing to happen in the past sennight.

Nay! She shouldn't… The last time she'd sworn she would not allow it to happen again. But… how she wanted his lips on hers… To mold against him. For wicked heat to wrap around her skin, his velvet tongue sliding along hers.

Aye… she did want this.

She licked her lower lip, prepared for when he reached for her. When his strong hand grazed her upper arm, she shivered. This was it… Anticipation made her heart kick up a notch. But just as suddenly as he'd touched her, he seemed to come to his senses and took a step back.

Elle cleared her throat, grateful (if a little disappointed) that he'd had the sense to back away from kissing her. Stay the course. That was what she needed to do. Not get distracted by a handsome warrior and his delicious mouth.

She straightened, hands on her hips and berated him. "Do ye often barge into a lady's bedchamber without knocking?"

"Nay." His voice was thick, gravelly, and sent a chill of desire racing over her spine. "Never."

Desire. She desired him. The sensation was new, heady, and left her searching for words, when all she wanted was to lie down and explore these feelings more wholly. "Then why did ye do so, just now? Ah-ha!" She narrowed her eyes and poked his chest. Good heavens, he was thick, hard with muscle. Elle forced herself not to concentrate on that aspect of him. Not to recall just how delicious and hard he felt pressed against her form. To pull back when she wanted to stroke. "Dinna answer that." Why was her voice so husky? She cleared her throat, something she'd been doing a lot around him. "Ye knew I was having a bath. 'Twas trickery!"

Beiste grinned slowly, the teasing glint in his eyes confirming her words even as he said, "Nay, nay, nay," and held up his hands. "That was not it at all. I simply…" He trailed off, eyes once more raking her length before he frowned and crossed his arms over his chest.

The man was having just as hard a time as her, and she found that marginally satisfying.

Elle watched a play of emotions come over his features that made her a little unsteady on her feet. What game was this he played? She enjoyed it and was scared all the same. She'd yet to discover the rules or the way to win. And what was the prize?

"Well, what is it?" she asked. Then, suddenly, the cobwebs of confusion were swept clean. "Wait, ye're *back*! Where is Erik?"

Now Beiste cleared his throat. He shifted his eyes to the side, unable to meet her gaze. "That is what I came to tell ye. May I come in?"

All the heat that had filled her blood pooled around her feet, replaced with an icy chill. "Nay. Just say it now." Her voice was breathless, her heart breaking at the thought of the darkest of news he could give her.

That shadowy darkness that had been on his face when she first met him clouded over his features. She knew without him having to say anything that Erik was not at Dunstaffnage. But what more? Had he found her brother? Any trace?

Elle backed up, shaking her head. "Nay. I willna believe it. Tell me ye found him!"

Beiste followed her into the room, reaching for her for a

brief moment before letting his hands fall at his sides. "I'm afraid Castle Gloom was abandoned. Not a soul in sight. Completely deserted. Cleaned up save for the ash as well."

Her parents' bodies... They'd likely buried the dead then.

"Glenna and Barra's croft was also burned out. I'm told the inhabitants escaped." This he said in a softer voice. "A young imp we found said no Erik had ever been there."

Young imp. Must have been Mary. She'd lied to keep Erik safe. That must mean that he'd escaped, too. Elle slicked her hands through her wet hair, grabbing the sides of her head as though that could stop the instant pounding she felt in her skull. Poor, Erik! She should not have left him. Oh, for the love of all that was holy, she prayed that Bjork had not found him.

"Nay..." she whispered. "How could this be?"

"Bjork and his men must have expected us. They abandoned the castle. I believe they've gone into the mountains. Hiding for now, waiting. Mayhap to set up a trap, or prepare for another siege. Here."

"And Erik? No one was at the castle? No sign of my brother?" Where could he have gone? Glenna and Barra had sworn that they would protect him. Was it possible they'd hidden him somewhere else?

Beiste's eyes flickered over her face. "Nay. No one."

Elle dropped to her knees, shaking. The floorboards blurred as tears filled her eyes. Great, racking sobs took hold of her body. She wasn't one to break down so easily, but when she'd abandoned her brother, thinking to make him safer, she'd never expected that he'd simply vanish. That she would have done better to just hand him over to the enemy herself. Sucking in a breath, she asked again, "Nothing?" and prayed he'd change his answer.

Beiste knelt on the floor in front of her. "Nay," he whispered. "I wish I could say there was."

Shocking both him and herself, Elle hauled off and punched him square in the chest, letting all her anger ride through that blow. Beiste barely budged, barely made a sound, didn't even try to stop her as she pummeled him some more. Working through the fury, the anguish. This was her fault Erik was missing. Until, finally, he grabbed hold of her, crushed her to him, her arms pinned to her sides. He stared into her eyes.

"Enough," he said softly.

Elle wriggled to get free, tears streaking down her cheeks.

"Enough," he said again, keeping one arm all the way around her to hold her own arms still.

With his free hand, he wiped at the tears tracking down her cheeks. His gaze roved over her, perhaps settling a little too long on her lips.

*Pray, kiss me.* If only to help her escape the pain that gripped her chest.

"I have failed him," she moaned, grabbing hold of his shirt.

Beiste caressed her face, staring into her eyes. "Och, lass, I know what that feels like. But ye didna fail him. Ye've done all that ye can."

"How?"

But instead of answering her, he brushed his lips over hers. Elle sighed at the sudden but gentle touch. The sensation sent a ripple over her skin, up and down her arms, heating her middle. The same awareness she'd had when he kissed her in the arbor, when he'd gazed on her nakedness intensified. Utterly spellbinding. She pressed her lips urgently to his, wanting to drink him in, to savor every velvet stroke.

Just as suddenly as he'd kissed her, he stopped, frowning down at her.

She opened her mouth to say something. To say she was

done crying, to say she needed to dry her hair or go for a walk, but then he was kissing her again. His mouth settled over hers, possessively. He cupped one side of her face, his arm wrapped around her loosened enough that she was able to move, to flatten her chest to his, to sink against him and pray he held her steady. He was warm, tender, not at all the usual beast.

This time, when her hands started to tremble, it wasn't from weakness or fear. Nay, it was from excitement. Passion. Intrigue.

Elle sighed, leaning closer, her hands fisting in his shirt. She tilted her head, wanting more of his thrilling kiss. More of the madness it brought her, the interruption from her pain. Beiste responded with an intensity that sent a shock jolting through her. He swiped his tongue over hers, nibbled at her lips until she was sighing with pleasure, a limp mass of heated flesh and desire.

"Bloody hell," he growled, separating himself from her.

She gazed up at him in confusion, his face full of thunder.

"What...?" she asked, somewhat bemused.

"I shouldna be doing this... Again," he said through bared teeth. Beiste climbed to his feet, taking with him the heat, the thrill. "I failed to find your brother, to find Bjork, but I am not done. I will continue to search for him. I only returned for reinforcements."

Elle swallowed, feeling grateful that he wouldn't stop his search, but also extremely confused about what had just happened. Did he not enjoy kissing her? If not, why did he keep doing it?

She touched her swollen, tingly lips as he retreated from the room.

For being new at kissing, she'd thought it had gone rather quite well until he'd started growling. Until he'd stormed away—*again*.

The blasted man was so confusing.

Och, who was she kidding? She was just as equally confused.

And the last thing she needed to be worrying about was kissing when Erik was still missing.

## 11

*B*eiste stormed out of the castle, down to the lower bailey. His blood pumped passionately, thickly, through his veins. Thank the saints for his thick plaid and sporran, else everyone in the castle would see just how hot the lass made him.

Saints but he'd been ready to bed her right there on the damned floor. To make love to her. To take her to the heights of pleasure she'd never experienced. And to bury himself, his pain, his past, all between her thighs, in a moment of sheer, blinding passion.

Beiste hadn't made love to a woman since he'd lost his wife three years before. A long time for any man. And it was apparent his body was ready to get back into the game, even if his mind was not.

"Gunnar," he bellowed. "Bring me the new recruits."

He was going to beat the men to bloody hell in the name of training and his own sanity. Exorcise his demons. Push past the feral need that had gripped him since opening the door and letting the dripping wet vixen into his castle.

A little over two hours later, sweat covered his entire

body, dripping in rivulets. He'd stripped out of his shirt, letting the cool air stroke briskly over his heated skin. Muscles tired, men laying on the ground all around him, sore, a little wounded, and all of them just as winded.

But, still, he kept staring up at the castle, his mind wandering back to the delicious kisses he'd shared with Elle. The images of just what he wanted to teach her. He was fairly certain she'd never kissed a man before him. Or else anyone she'd kissed had been just as inexperienced as she. There was something heady and powerful about that. That he could be the one to introduce her to pleasure. That she could be the one to pull him from his informal vow of celibacy.

*Ballocks!* What in bloody hell was he thinking? She wasn't a light skirt! She was a lady. A virgin for blood's sake. Not a lass to be trifled with. Not a lass he could bed and forget. Nay, the only way he'd be doing anymore kissing, let alone bedding, with Lady Elle Cam'béal was if she was Lady Elle *MacDougall*. And that bloody well wasn't going to happen. He wasn't ready to marry again. And he never would be.

"Och," he growled, shoving his way through his men. "I'm going for a swim. The lot of ye stinking bastards might as well join me."

They followed him to the shore, diving into the chilly water and scooping up sand to scrub away the sweat from their bodies.

"Son…"

Beiste jerked his head out of the water where he'd been dunking to give his hair a wash.

"What the…" He looked around, swearing he'd just heard his father call out to him.

Damn it to hell. His father was dead. Sent off over the water on a great funeral pyre. Beiste had helped carry the litter, had ordered the flaming arrows to light the kindling, and watched until his father's boat sank into the horizon.

"Son." The voice was stronger now.

Beiste swiveled in the water, not seeing anyone around him. His men had climbed to the shore, going back to their duties. Was this a bloody jest? Was one of them purposefully trying to goad him? Beiste kicked out at the water, hoping to catch whoever it was in the jaw.

No one there.

"Beiste, my son." The voice could have been one inch from his ear.

And yet he was alone. Which meant only one thing: his mind was the one playing tricks on him.

"Get out of my head," Beiste growled, marching swiftly through the water toward the shore.

As soon as he stepped onto the sand, a shadow fell over him. He felt a prickle wind its way up his spine. But still, there was no one there. He drew his sword, turning in a circle. Partially grateful his men had returned to their duties, so as not to witness his momentary lapse in sanity.

"Who is there?"

He half-expected to hear his father's voice again but, instead, the lad he'd brought back from Castle Gloom climbed from behind a bush.

"What are ye doing back there? Always hiding." Beiste's voice was a little gruffer than he would have liked, but he was still irritated with the apparent voice in his head and his desire for a certain half-Scot, half-Viking minx.

John was wringing his hands, a task he'd taken to doing anytime he was around Beiste. He shifted his gaze from Beiste to the sea. "I'm sorry, my laird. I but…wondered if I might have a swim to get clean, too?"

The imp was caked with grime, and smelled horrendous. "Och, aye. I should have thought of it sooner. Jump in." Beiste finished dressing while the lad scrubbed himself the same as the men had.

When he climbed out, he had a smile on his face. Black hair clung wet to his forehead, his skin smooth and white. Piercing blue eyes met his. Again, Beiste had a flash of knowing. The lad looked so familiar to him, yet he knew they'd never met before, he was certain. Perhaps, his merchant parents had come by the castle, once.

"Are ye hungry, lad?"

"Aye."

Beiste clapped him on the shoulder, catching him as the mighty thwack sent the lad tumbling forward. "Sorry about that, forgot how tiny ye were. Come, let's get ye a change of clothes and something to eat in the kitchens. Ye can sleep in the stables tonight with the other grooms, unless ye prefer the great hall. Might be a touch warmer in there."

John beamed up at him, straightening his shoulders. "I love horses."

"Oh, do ye now?"

"Aye."

"Can ye ride?"

"Aye. My father taught me."

That was impressive. Not many merchant's children learned how to ride. Most of them worked themselves to the bones. And judging from the lad's clothes when they'd found him, he was surprised that John's father would have access to a horse. Possibly, he'd only learned to ride on the mule that would have dragged the wagon. In any case, Beiste didn't want to lesson the lad's pride in his ability. "Then ye'll be a good addition to Master Collins."

"I want to thank ye for taking me in." The boy ran a hand through his wet mane. "Do ye often take in strangers?"

"Nay," Beiste said with a frown. "Not often." Save for lately, and all of them hailing from the same place it would seem. But he kept that truth to himself.

When the sun set that evening, Beiste could have sworn it was hours early, that darkness had won out over the light. Or perhaps, that was simply his mood.

The day had passed by quickly, despite his internal struggles, with preparations for their Viking hunt. The men and horses were rested and upon first light, they would, once more, journey toward Castle Gloom. Only this time, they would be searching the mountains for the villainous Bjork.

Beiste entered the great hall, prepared to sit at the table and eat the evening meal, but Elle was not present. His stomach rumbled as fiercely as his temper. Why did she toy with him? He'd specifically given orders for her to join him for supper in the great hall, so that all within the clan would see she was accepted by him, not a prisoner. Besides, having had musings of her and her luscious lips all day, imagining her body pressed to his, he thought it best to see her in person, to push those thoughts from his mind. To reinforce that she was not some sensual goddess, but a plain, ordinary woman.

*Bloody liar.*

Perhaps he'd over exaggerated the softness of her skin, the deep knowing wells of her beautiful eyes, or the lush curves of her body and plush red of her lips. His mind seemed to have made her into a deity throughout the day and he needed to prove himself wrong.

*Lies. Lies. Lies.*

"Mrs. Lach, where is the lady?" he demanded, trying not to roar out the question.

His housekeeper looked perplexed, pursing her lips and wiping her hands on her apron. Shifting her gaze toward the wall behind him, she said, "She is not coming down, my laird. She's said she willna be having supper this evening."

"Why?" he snapped, losing some control on the temper he kept tightly leashed. Didn't she realize this was for her own good?

"I dinna know. I didna ask."

Beiste grunted, turned on his heel and headed for the stairs. Mrs. Lach might not have asked, but he damned well would. When he gave an order, he expected it to be heeded. Men died for less.

Upon reaching her door, he paused, hand in mid-air. He'd not spoken to her the entire day. Not since their kiss. And from that, he'd left in a disgruntled temper. Probably hurt her feelings in the process. 'Twas no wonder she chose to remain in her chamber. He'd not meant to upset her and she should know better. Shouldn't she?

Women were supposed to be the ones who empathized with others, understood them, not the other way around. Why was he even having these thoughts? Aye, she should have come down at his invitation, no matter the way in which they'd parted. In fact, he was certain it was rude of her to have denied his request for her presence.

With that thought in mind, he raised his hand and pounded on the door.

"Who is it?" she called from within in a singsong voice. She'd been waiting for him, he was almost certain of it. A game she was playing.

Beiste rolled his eyes, wanting to simply walk in, but after what had happened that morning…seeing all that white, creamy flesh as she'd stood from her bath. Beiste closed his eyes, pressed his lips together and counted to ten. His blood pumped ardently, and it took everything he had not to crash through the door and stake his claim. Hell, he couldn't make the visions vanish. Next time, he'd be unable to control himself. And he imagined reaching for her, pressing his hard frame to her soft, naked, wet curves…zounds, but his body was reacting powerfully. Growing hot, hard with need. He wanted her. Needed her.

Like he'd never wanted or needed another.

Not even his beloved.

Saints, but was he betraying his wife's memory by having these thoughts, feelings, reactions to another? Nay! Men lost wives and took new ones all the time. He wasn't so different. Besides, on her deathbed, his wife had demanded he move on, and that was what his people expected, too. But to do so meant risking more lives.

Aye, he felt guilty for it. Guilty for what would happen should he allow his feelings for this young chit to sink in and truly take hold. He'd be the death of her. Just like everyone else.

"Come to the great hall," he demanded to the wooden planks of the door.

"Nay, thank ye," she called, not bothering to open the barrier.

Beiste let out a low growl of frustration. "'Tis not a request."

That had her opening the door, fast enough to cause a breeze to swirl around the hem of her blue wool gown. His wife's gown…

Beiste was silent. Speechless.

He took a step back, afraid for his own reaction.

Aye, he'd told Mrs. Lach to give the clothes to his guest, but he'd never imagined they would look so fine on her. The soft fabric clung to her curves. Over her shoulder, he spied the MacDougall sash that should have gone from one shoulder to her waist was laid carefully at the foot of her bed. His nostrils flared as a swift vision of her wrapped in nothing but his plaid assailed him.

*Ballocks!*

"Ye…" His mouth grew dry and he couldn't finish speaking. She looked even more beautiful than he remembered. The color of the wool brought out the green of her eyes. Made her hair all the more vibrant. Her skin creamy, as though she'd been formed of milk and honey.

But the frown, the downward curve of those haughty lips. Perhaps that's what drew him to her all the more. Lady Elle wasn't afraid of him. Wasn't afraid to speak her mind with him.

"I thank ye for the *demand*, sir, but I am not hungry. And I dinna feel like celebrating when my brother is likely starving or beaten somewhere."

Beiste narrowed his eyes, trying for intimidating. "Do ye plan to starve yourself along with him? Might I remind ye that ye were fainting not to long ago from hunger? What good are ye to your people if the both of ye end up dead?"

Elle frowned, delicate hands going to her hips, mouth pursed. Lord, but that was dangerous. He wanted to kiss her. Again. And again. And again.

Take her swiftly into his arms and claim those pouty red lips for his own.

*Nay*! Not for his own. Bloody *not* his!

Beiste scraped his hands through his hair, over his trimmed beard, deciding perhaps it was best for her to remain up here with the door closed and temptation at bay. "Suit yourself," he fairly growled, then whirled on his heel. Before he'd made it three feet, he tossed over his shoulder, "The gown is verra becoming on ye."

The nearly inaudible gasp she let out made his chest swell and that only irritated him more. He'd surprised her with his compliment. A compliment he should only have paid her if she'd decided to heed his demands. But it seemed he was constantly astonishing himself around her.

Beiste stormed down the corridor to the stairs, taking them two at a time until he was back in the great hall, slamming himself into his chair and working hard not to growl.

He waved to the servants to begin bringing the trenchers out. The trestle tables were filled with his men and people of the clan. Even wee John had joined them, eating a few timid bites with the other stable lads before being ushered out by the stable master.

With every bite, Beiste swigged a sip of ale, tasteless, though he knew from experience his cook was very talented. His mind was on the woman upstairs. The enemy that lay in wait in the mountains. The mystery of the sword and how she'd come to be in possession of it. He'd not felt he could ask her about it without first returning her brother to her as had been his promise. And every time he was with her, his thoughts took a decidedly different route.

There was also the fact that her father had been The Irish. Had the man stolen the sword from Beiste's father?

And just where the bloody hell had Erik Cam'béal gone? Was he with Bjork? Buried along with any other casualties? Running the hills and hiding much like young John had been?

When he'd finished eating, Beiste waved Mrs. Lach to him. "I need another trencher."

She nodded and returned swiftly with one. He filled it with food, poured another cup of wine, and stood up, heading for the stairs. If the lass wouldn't come down, then he was going to bring her food. Couldn't have her starve even if she insisted she wasn't hungry. Her brother, whenever the man was found, would not take kindly to his sister being half-starved.

Juggling the trencher and cup on one arm, he knocked, gently this time, with the other.

She opened the door a moment later, peeking out at him through the two-inch crack. He was glad to see she was surprised to spy him with the trencher and wine.

"I brought ye supper."

The door opening widened and she stared at the fare with hunger in her eyes. He'd known she was famished, no matter if she wanted to make a martyr of herself. The lass had an appetite like no other female he'd seen and he found he liked watching her eat.

"Ye like to see me fed," she mumbled, as if reading his thoughts. Elle eyed him warily, perhaps trying to judge if he was going to require any sort of payment for his kindness.

Beiste ground his teeth. "'Tis my duty to see that all in my charge are well-cared for."

"Is that what I am? In your charge?"

Beiste sighed, so much for keeping temptation at bay. He just couldn't stay away. Nudging past her to place the food and drink on the table, he said, "Ye're my guest, as I've stated. Ye have free reign of the castle and grounds. And aye, as long as ye're under my roof, ye're in my charge, my responsibility. I will be certain ye are well. Beyond that, my father made an oath to your family. I will see that the oath is kept." *And I will try my damndest not to sweep ye up in my arms again. Heaven help me...*

"I'm sorry," she said softly, twirling a long tendril of her hair around her finger. "I'm verra grateful for all ye've done. I dinna know why I am so angry. Ye're not my enemy. Ye've made that... clear..." A heady rose color flushed along her neck and cheeks.

She was thinking of their kisses, he was certain. The same thing was never far from his mind either.

Beiste came closer to her, unable to help touching her cheek. She was soft, warm. He jerked his fingers back, only wanting to touch her more.

"I'm not." His throat was tight. He wanted to kiss her again and if she—

She looked up at him, eyes wide, lips parted. Lord help him. He ground his teeth to keep from wrapping his arms around her.

"I confess, I'm lost, my laird," she said.

Lost. Lost just like him. Mind floating in a chaos of emotion, confusion, need. "Call me Beiste."

"Beiste..." She swallowed, the little nob in her throat rising and falling. "Thank ye."

"Ye dinna need to thank me."

"I do. I only hope that one day I can repay the kindness ye've shown me. Restore something ye've lost."

His chest clenched, fingers tightened into fists as the pain of his past came to the forefront, reminding him of why he couldn't have her. "I have lost everyone."

"Not everyone." Her lips hitched slightly in the corners. "There are many within these walls who love ye, who respect ye."

Saints, but he was finding it hard to speak. No one had been able to elicit such emotion from him and he'd barely uttered more than a few words. But the words, the darkness and deepness of them. They were the very essence of his soul, the very thing he feared. Why had he felt compelled to confess to her? Och, but it hadn't been a choice. The words had slipped out before he'd even had a chance to rein them in. This was *her*. All her. She had the ability to open him up wide without his realizing it. No one else before her had this effect. Why was she so different? How was she able to get inside of his head?

Beiste swallowed around the thickness of his throat and when he spoke, his words sounded gruff, muted almost. "Aye. Ye're right."

"But that's not what ye meant was it?" she asked, her eyes imploring, searching his for some meaning he couldn't grasp.

"Nay."

"Your father and mother, they are looking down on ye now. Just as I hope mine are looking down on me."

"Aye." Saints, but he needed to leave. He was getting hot. His chest tight. He felt backed into a corner and, yet, it seemed the only way out, the only way to escape his pain, his demons, was through *her*.

"Who else have ye lost?" She shook her head, her finger-tips momentarily brushing his arm. "Dinna answer that. 'Tis none of my business."

But once more, his lips were moving before his mind could stop him. "My brothers and sisters. My wife and...child."

Pain tore at his ribs. He'd never spoken of this to anyone.

"Oh..." Elle breathed out, her eyes glistening with unshed sentiment. "I'm so sorry to hear that. I had no idea." She stepped a little closer, her fingers brushing his arm. "The loss of loved ones so dear, that is a pain that does not wane. 'Tis unexpected. A hard ache to live with."

Beiste's heart clenched painfully. He didn't want to talk about them anymore. About the loss. The pain that he felt every damned day because of it. So instead, he did the next best thing. He slid his hands up her arms and tugged her against him, lowering his face toward hers. He stared into her eyes. Searching. Wanting. Desiring. Needing her to take away his pain.

"Lord, but ye are perfect. So beautiful. I need to kiss ye, Elle. I need to leave this place, these thoughts, and take ye with me. Will ye let me?"

She nodded, her eyelids fluttering closed.

Beiste wrapped her up in his arms and pressed his lips to hers, breathing in her floral scent, tasting the sweetness of her lips, glorying in the way her body molded so perfectly to his. The way her kiss, her touch, all of her, worked an enchantment to lessen his pain.

But at what cost?

What was he doing kissing her again? Bloody hell it felt so good...made him feel alive again. For so long he'd been lost. Dead. A man hidden by shadows, darkness that he wrapped around himself.

How easily he'd opened up to her and allowed in the light...

Damn cost! Damn pain! He wanted to be alive! He wanted to live again. Elle was making it happen, if only for a few fleeting moments. Could it be something that lasted longer? Could he allow himself to fall?

*Nay, dammit!* He couldn't let himself forget the losses. He wouldn't allow himself to put her in danger. Everyone he'd ever loved had been stripped from him. He could not allow that to be her fate, simply by falling for her. Simply by—

*Loving her?*

Nay. This wasn't love. Couldn't be and, yet, his heart swelled to an intense ache.

He'd confessed things to his first wife out of obligation, but never to any other woman. However with Elle, he felt he could share things from deep in his heart, that she would see him, know him, accept him. She was the light in his darkness.

"Blast," he growled against her mouth, tearing himself away. "I must go. We leave at first light."

"Be well, Beiste." Her parting words were shadowed in her own emotion. Sadness, loss.

*Mo chreach*, but he wasn't ready to dive down into those pools. Yet, he feared he'd already taken the plunge.

"*I* want to join ye."

Beiste stared down at the young lad who stood, feet spread at attention, hands fisted at his sides. Wee John had the bearings of a warrior, and would make a loyal retainer when he was of age.

"I admire your spirit, lad, but I canna allow ye to accompany us. Stay here, help the stable master. Keep the horses well cared for. Without horses, we warriors would be missing part of ourselves."

John's frown deepened. "I *need* to go. The man ye're after, he killed my parents. 'Tis my right."

Dismounting, Beiste approached the lad and pressed a hand to his shoulder. "Trust me when I say I know just what ye mean. But if I were to let ye go, and with no training, then your parents would haunt me until the end of my days."

That did not seem to faze John. "My father would be proud of me."

Beiste shook his head. "Your father would want ye to live." Patting the tiny shoulder, he continued, "Ye've many years to come yet that ye can prove yourself. Work hard,

ELIZA KNIGHT

train hard, and stay alive, so that when ye've grown into manhood, ye'll be the man your mother and father envisioned ye to be. That is unless they envisioned ye being a wool merchant. In that case, ye may want to spend time with the shepherd's to gain a better appreciation for your product."

John shook his head. "They knew I would never be a merchant."

Beiste could practically hear the lad's unspoken words: *I was born for greatness.*

He'd thought similarly when he was young. Thank goodness he'd not known the true meaning of his greatness—infinite sorrow.

There was only one light in the shadowy box he inhabited and that was Lady Elle.

"I must be off, lad. I trust ye'll do what is expected of ye?"

John gave a curt nod, the hard press of his lip doing little to hide the slight quiver. He'd learn soon enough.

Beiste mounted his charger once more and gave the signal for his men that it was time to leave. They rode through the gates and over the moors, crossing the River Awe at its shallow end and then River Orchy. They followed the path of the River Lochy through the mountains, passing over Ben Lui, Ben More and finally Ben Vorlich where Beiste was certain Bjork and his men had been.

Beiste dismounted to examine the abandoned camp. Standing in the center, he let out a growl and stabbed his sword into the rocky ground of the mountaintop. Here was all the evidence that he was once more too late. Cleared space where bodies had slept. Bones of animals they'd cooked littered the ground. Several campfires were fresh, but not lit. And not a single, damned Viking, outlaw or scrambling animal was in sight. The whoresons had eaten every last rabbit and tamped out their fires before rushing off.

He let out a curse and stabbed at the ground again. Frustrating was an understatement. The rage he felt at being one step behind these bastards was palpable. Beiste knelt and placed his hands over the ashes, gripping a half-burned log letting the dulled heat sink into his palm. The fires had been put out for perhaps two hours at most. They'd just missed them.

Probably their scouts had spotted Beiste and his men despite their efforts to remain silent and hidden. *Sassenachs* were easy to fool, easy to beat. Vikings however, they were on even playing ground with.

The number of rises in the mountain left plenty of places higher up in order to snoop. But why didn't they engage? Why were they running? Every experience he'd ever had with the Norsemen had been violent. They didn't run, they attacked. They didn't hide from their enemies but made themselves known. The bastards were not acting as he expected them to. They were unpredictable and Beiste didn't like that.

"Dealing with damned shadows," Beiste growled.

"Look at this." Gunnar held aloft a piece of plaid.

"Cam'béal colors." Beiste took the fabric in hand. It was small and torn. Either deliberately left behind or torn on something. "Could be any number of prisoners', but could also be Laird Erik's."

"Aye."

Beiste climbed back on his horse and circled the camp. "They've got horse tracks going in every direction, trying to confuse us. We'll have to split up."

The whoresons could try and evade him, but eventually they would be caught. Come hell or high water, Beiste was going to do as he'd vowed to Elle, and that was get Erik back.

But chasing Vikings soon seemed an undertaking easier said than done, for the next two days, they chased ghosts along the ridges and valleys of the mountain. And never once came face to face.

~

SLEEP EVADED ELLE.

Confusion ruled every inch of her darkened chamber. She would have gladly welcomed a visit from the old ghostly laird, if only to ask for an explanation of his son's behavior. And maybe even her own feelings.

Staring up at the darkened canopy above her, she allowed her mind to wander, returning frequently to her worry for Beiste and his men. Though he must know who he was going up against, Elle wasn't certain that he was fully prepared for the violence, or the lack of mercy, her relations would show. Elle was ashamed to even think of them as her relations.

There was no chivalry. No attempting to negotiate. It was kill or die. A motto they adhered to with a bloodthirsty vigor.

And Erik... If he wasn't hiding, then he had to be dead. Bjork would not leave her brother alive. She knew that deep in her heart. The way he'd crushed her parents without even waiting for them to issue a plea or bargain...

Mingling with her fear was a maelstrom of other emotions and visions of Beiste standing before her. Beiste reaching for her. Beiste's mouth descending toward hers. His wicked grin. The way he raised his brow at her and grinned.

What was she going to do about him? She pushed back the end of her question—*if he returns...* He would return. He just had to. There was no room for doubt in her mind.

Whenever she thought of Beiste a warm cloud enveloped her. A sense of rightness. An awareness of being home. Her heart quickened, and tears sprang to her eyes.

"Return to me," she whispered to the dark. "Bring Erik back. Let us all rejoice together."

Elle swiped at the wetness on her face, recalling how Beiste had wiped her tears. How gentle he was and yet also so very passionate.

Every kiss had been divine bliss. Every caress made her yearn for more. But even beyond the physical side, were the emotions, the *feelings*. He'd opened his heart to her, let her inside to see his darkest fears. The vulnerable side of him, and oh how she'd wanted to pick up the pieces of his heart and smooth them back together.

But he'd pushed her away.

For the briefest of moments, part of her had wondered if by kissing her, he was taking himself back in time. Remembering his wife. But then the other part of her, the part that saw into his eyes, the way he held her gaze, the intensity there, she knew he was kissing *her*.

She could be his healing touch.

Beiste was rough and gruff on the outside, but underneath, she knew the true heart inside of him. And what was more terrifying, she wanted to explore that heart. See how deep he'd let her go.

Elle shivered, running her hands along her limbs, her heart swelling with an emotion she found both terrifying and exhilarating. *Love.* 'Twas as if her soul reached out for his.

Was this some magical spell? A trick of the fairies? Their way of convincing her she was meant to protect the lands of both families as the *glaistig*? Forcing her to fall in love? Unable to give up the man she loved?

Well, she wasn't going to fall for that. *Nay*!

If she was doomed to walk the earth for eternity, then she'd damned well *choose* who she was going to love.

They couldn't force that on her. Wasn't that some kind of mystical law? *Thou shalt not force love…* She could imagine all the fairies standing around their sparkling, magical court as their leader shouted the commandment. The silly thought made her smile. Aye, they couldn't force her to do anything she didn't want to. To feel anything she didn't of her own free will.

Problem was…she couldn't stop thinking of Beiste, his kisses, his mesmerizing eyes and the sweet gifts he continued to give her. The way she felt in his arms, or the way her heart flipped with he was near. Everything she'd felt for him was real, had to be.

When sleep finally came to her, she dreamt of him, too…

## 14

$T$he sound of horses thundering close to the gate jerked Elle from her momentary reverie. She lifted her head from where she'd bent to pick a sprig of rosemary in the herb garden and listened.

Her heart kicked up a notch, her neck growing tingly.

*Beiste. Erik.*

The men had been gone for eight days. During that time, she'd finally ventured from her room to explore a bit of the castle grounds, finding most of her peace in the gardens among the fragrant herbs, flowers and vegetables. The only thing she'd not been able to do that she desperately wanted was to take a ride. She longed to feel the wind in her hair. The sleek muscles of a horse beneath her as they moved as one across the landscape. But before she could even reach the stables, one of the guards always stepped into her path, claiming that denying her a ride was for her own safety. Master's orders.

Well, he was probably right with the enemy still being out there, but still… That didn't make her want it any less.

Elle had been forced to find other pursuits to occupy her

time. Anything to distract herself from thoughts of Beiste, the fairies and fears for her brother.

But the sounds of riders, that was unmistakable. Even if she stuck her head into the dirt, she'd not be able to escape it. The ground fairly rumbled beneath her feet from the force of the horses' pounding.

Lifting the hem of the deep green gown she'd been gifted with, she ran around the side of the castle toward the bailey.

The gates were opened by the men on guard and she chewed her lip, bouncing on her feet in her anticipation. Erik had to be with Beiste this time.

As the men filed through, she searched their faces, looked for her brother's slight body amongst them. With each passing horse, her stomach knotted tighter and her jaw clenched harder. Rigid warrior faces stared back at her, their gazes unnerving, the disappointment palpable.

When Beiste rode through the gate last, her fears came to a head.

No Erik.

No prisoners.

No signs of blood on their garments—no battle?

The expression on Beiste's face said it all. Their mission had been a failure. Bjork was still out there. Her brother was still out there. With every passing moment, the chance of Erik surviving decreased.

All the time she'd spent thinking about Beiste, his kisses, dreaming of a chance at something more, and her brother was still missing. She was a fool, and she'd laid her trust in a man who couldn't or wouldn't come through for her.

Elle felt as though she might explode. Anger pummeled her insides. Turned her blood hotter than a flame. The same guilty sentiments she'd chanted through her mind like a mantra the last fortnight reared their ugly heads. *You should never have left him! This is your fault!*

Why had she entrusted virtual strangers for the care of her brother, and another for his return? Just because Beiste's father had been a trustworthy and dedicated ally did not mean that Beiste would be.

Beiste didn't even know what her brother looked like, let alone the places in which he would hide. She'd been a fool to give a task that clearly belonged to her, over to another. And more a fool still for not having given him the information he would have needed to locate her brother.

"Ye didna find him," she said, unable to hide the upset in her voice.

Beiste shook his head slightly. Dismounted, and started to approach her. Elle held up her hands, shaking her head and took several steps back.

"Ye promised!" Her voice was growing shrill, hysterics threatening to take hold, and she was powerless to keep them from coming.

"My lady—"

"Nay! No more of your promises. No more of your useless declarations. I should never have come here. I should never have asked for your help."

She didn't wait for him to reply, but whirled on her heels and ran toward the castle, up the stairs. Nearly two weeks had passed since she'd left Castle Gloom. Time was not a luxury she possessed. Her brother needed her and needed her now.

For the first time since Bjork had shattered her life, she was going to take control and do what she should have done in the beginning.

Elle pushed through her chamber door and whirled in a circle. What was she even doing up here? She didn't own anything, not even the gown she wore. At least the boots and mantle were hers. Flinging open the wardrobe, she rifled through the contents until she found her own gown that

Mrs. Lach had been kind enough to have washed and Elle had herself repaired the tears. She quickly stripped out of the soft wool gown she'd been given and pulled on her own.

There was only one way to get her brother back and that was to sacrifice herself.

She grunted, finding the irony of it all too deep.

A blood sacrifice. Only, she'd be giving herself over to the Vikings in order to save her young brother.

And if what the old laird said was true, she'd live a life of misery with Bjork only to haunt Beiste and his descendants for eternity.

A daunting realization. One that sucked the air from her lungs, made her double over to catch her breath.

But it didn't change things.

She'd stand atop the mountain that looked down upon Castle Gloom and she'd shout for Bjork to come out of the shadows. For him to take what he'd come for and let her people go. Let Erik go. She'd demand that he and his horde of monsters leave Scotland and return to their northern territory. And maybe, she'd leap from the bow of their ship and sink into the depths of the cold sea.

"Where are ye going?" 'Twas the voice of the ghost laird.

So used to his presence, Elle didn't even bother to search for the vision of him. "To make a sacrifice. Isn't that what ye want?"

There was a whisper of cold touch down her arm and she glanced up to see his face floating before her, wrinkled and transparent, concerned all the same.

He nodded. "Ye'll need the sword."

"Do ye know where it is?" she asked, not having seen it since she'd arrived.

"Aye."

"Take me." She followed the ghost through the door in her

chamber that led into Beiste's room. The sword was placed carefully on metal hooks, mounted on the wall above his headboard. "He has no idea what that sword represents," Elle mused.

"Ye will tell him, eventually."

"Nay, I dinna think I'll have the chance." Elle reached up, running her fingers over the jeweled hilt. How many times had her father, brother, done that very same thing? Somehow, with the sword, she felt a connection to them, if only in memory.

When no reply came from the old laird, she looked to her side to see she was, once more, alone. Elle reached for the heavy sword with both hands, taking it off the metal hooks and hoisting it into the air. The blasted thing weighed a ton. A sword for a mighty warrior. As strong as she liked to think she was, the sword was nearly as tall as she was. Escape would be made harder. When she'd left Barra's croft, she'd been lucky to have a horse right away, not a prospect she expected to have this time around. Her journey would be arduous.

Elle searched through the chest at the foot of Beiste's bed, her heart pounding, sweat breaking out along her spine. She'd spent too much time up here. He was bound to come searching for her soon. Or at the very least, perhaps clean himself up in his own chamber.

At the bottom of the chest, she found what she was looking for. The MacDougall/Cam'béal baldric. She adjusted the straps to fit, slid the sword into the sheath and then hooked it in place on her back. With the hilt rising above her head and the tip nearly to the back of her knees, she'd have to be careful not to cut herself while running.

There was no more time to waste. Any minute Beiste could come searching for her.

Elle stepped out into the corridor, fearful that she'd run

right into Beiste, one of his guards or a servant. Fortunately, all was silent, except for the old laird who was back.

"This way," he whispered, waving a luminous arm.

Elle followed him down the stairs, through winding corridors that grew darker and darker, until he pointed to a secret door she never would have known existed. She pushed the door open, seeing that it led out into the woods, then paused.

"Why are ye helping me?"

"Ye need it."

Elle shook her head. "But dinna ye want me to stay here? To be with Beiste?"

The ghost winked. "Sometimes ye need to be the ripple. Be safe, my dear one."

She smiled up at him, feeling a sudden pulse of righteousness in her chest. An armor of hope. "Thank ye for your kindness, in this form and in the past."

"Is Fate a kindness?" His figure faded before she could answer him, but his words remained in her mind, left her questioning just that.

Elle pulled her mantle up over her head and ran deeper into the woods.

BEISTE HANDED HIS REINS TO JOHN WHO'D HURRIED FROM THE stables after Elle had fled inside.

"Who was the lady?" John asked, his gaze downcast, but the interest full in his voice, his cheeks flushed with color.

Beiste dismounted and patted young John on his head. "A guest of mine." He trudged toward the keep, needing very badly to speak with his *guest*.

But the lad chased after him. "What is her name?"

Beiste stopped in his tracks, hands on his hips and faced

the scamp. "Dinna concern yourself with women, lad. Ye've many years to go afore ye need worry over them."

"I dinna, my laird." John was wringing his hands again. "I, well, I thought I recognized her voice." The lad sounded almost forlorn.

Beiste squinted his eyes, staring at his features. The way his shoulders sagged. He supposed the lad could recognize her voice if he'd been at Castle Gloom. Maybe he was looking for the comfort of someone familiar. But then, the lad met his gaze again. Though his shoulders were slumped, his skin taut with tension over his face, his eyes were strong, fierce. There was a determination behind them that Beiste had not seen before. Suddenly, a thought struck him. Could it be? Had he been so incredibly wrong this entire time?

"Bloody hell," Beiste growled. Only one way to find out. "Erik?"

The imp's eyes widened and he turned to flee, but Beiste grabbed him by the scruff of his neck and whirled him around.

"Answer me, lad. Are ye Erik Cam'béal?"

"Aye," he squeaked.

Beiste saw red. Anger sliced through his limbs. "Do ye know we've been riding all over the godforsaken land looking for ye?" Why hadn't anyone bothered to tell him the laird they were looking for was a wee lad? Beiste could have bellowed, could have pummeled a man into the ground. But, somehow, he managed to rein in his temper.

"They said ye were looking for the Viking." Erik's voice had grown stronger, though there was still a bit of a quiver. "Bjork. The murderer."

"*And* ye! Your sister came here begging for my help."

"So the lady *is* Elle." John—er Erik's—head swiveled toward the castle, completely unconcerned with having put men's lives in danger.

"Are ye hearing me, lad?" Beiste said through gritted teeth.

"Aye. Let me see her." There was no question in his demand, but an order. From a lad.

Beiste laughed. "Ye may be a laird, young pup, but ye're on my land. And the only reason ye've a castle to your name is because of my father."

Erik's gaze burned back on his. "My castle. Ye claimed it. Ye'll return it to me."

"Aye, but not until ye're ready."

That had the little scamp growing red in the face, his own teeth bared, fists clenched, giving Beiste the impression that when he was a man, he'd be a mighty one to be reckoned with. "What right do ye have?"

"I am your overlord. I have every right."

"I want to see my sister. *Now.*" Erik stomped his foot.

Rather than cause a scene, Beiste rolled his eyes and said, "All right. And I suppose ye'll not want to be sleeping in the stables anymore?"

Erik straightened, hands fisted at his sides. "Nay."

"Why did ye lie to me?" Beiste leveled his gaze on the lad, daring him to lie again.

"For my protection. For Elle's."

"But ye didna need protection from me. I was the one helping ye."

Erik shrugged. "How was I to know to trust ye just yet?"

Beiste sighed. "Ye're right. I'd have done the same thing. Come now. Let us get the two of ye reunited." And to cease the frigid glares Elle was certain to toss his way.

Och, frigid... Devastated was more like it.

When he'd come through the gate and seen her staring at him as though he'd truly betrayed her, it had torn at Beiste's heart. She'd been the only thing keeping him going the past sennight while they searched the mountains. He dreamt of her at night and fantasized about her during the day. Wanted to make her happy, to take away the pain that had been caused to her over the past weeks. Not to be the one to give her more.

That had to be why he'd let her rail at him in front of the entire clan. Speechless he'd been, and rightly cowed by her ire. She had every right to be so angry. Lord, she was going to be thrilled when she saw her brother safe and sound.

Beiste led Erik into the castle and up the stairs to Elle's chamber. The door was ajar, but still he knocked with the back of his knuckles, not wanting to push into her chamber the way he had before—when she'd been in the bath. Blast it... But he could still see her in that tub. This was not the time, nor the company, in which to start thinking of sweet Elle soaking wet and naked.

When she did not answer, Beiste knocked again. "My lady? I've a visitor for ye."

Still nothing. Where Beiste hesitated, Erik did not. The young pup pushed past him and shoved the door wide.

"Elle! Do ye not care to see me—" Erik cut himself off short at seeing the chamber was empty.

Beiste frowned. "She's not here," he grumbled, stating the obvious.

Having not been home the past several days, he wasn't certain where else she'd be, but he knew someone who did. "The housekeeper ought to know where she is."

They trudged back down the stairs to the kitchens, finding the heated room to be all a bustle with preparations for the noon meal.

"Mrs. Lach?" he called.

She stepped from the buttery. "Aye, my laird?"

"Have ye seen Lady Elle?"

Mrs. Lach carried a tub of lard to the center table. "She's in her chamber, my laird."

"Nay, she's not."

The housekeeper frowned, issuing an order to one of the scullions. "I saw her go up there myself. Havena seen her come down."

"She's not there, I assure ye."

"Check the gardens."

And so it went. They searched the gardens, the stables, every chamber in the massive keep, every well, storehouse and merchant's outbuilding. Every crofter's hut. No sign of her.

"She's gone," Erik said accusingly. "What did ye say to her to make her leave?"

"I didna say naught." Beiste had a feeling it wasn't what he'd said necessarily—but the lack of what he'd been able to do for her. His failure to return her brother, except, dammit, he'd already done just that! Over a sennight ago!

"Then 'haps that's what forced her away. Ye said naught."

Beiste ground his teeth, not wanting to get into an argument with the lad, and feeling the need to rage all the same. "How could saying naught have made her leave?"

"Ye know nothing about women." Erik shook his head and if Beiste hadn't been on the edge of losing his temper, he might have laughed at how the roles seemed to be reversed.

But he was at the very precipice of madness and rage. Hands fisted at his sides, he bellowed a war cry, punched the wattle and daub wall of the croft, leaving a massive dent, and let out a string of curses.

Who knew that the simple act of finding her gone would leave him so bereft? So angry? So lost…

Beiste grabbed up a bucket, flinging it over a hundred feet, then kicked a stone, ready to punch anyone who got in his way.

"My laird." Gunnar's stern voice was a wake-up call and

Beiste glanced up to see his second-in-command staring him down. "We'll find her."

Beiste nodded, apologizing to the crofter whose house he'd just damaged, promising to see if repaired.

Only Gunnar knew the extent of his pain. Not that he'd ever told him, but the man had been around long enough to figure it out.

Another person he…cared about had gone missing. Beiste couldn't bring himself to say how he really felt, for he'd only just realized it with the gut-wrenching that had torn through him. He was utterly, madly, deeply in love with Elle Cam'béal and she'd left him. Hadn't believed in him.

"Stubborn wench," Beiste growled.

Erik grunted. "Now ye're starting to understand."

Gunnar placed a firm grip on Beiste's shoulder when he lurched forward to grapple the young laird.

"Best be keeping your opinions to yourself, lad," Gunnar warned Erik.

Erik crossed his thin arms over his narrow chest. A lad, who had several years before he'd grow into a man. "I'm coming with ye."

"Like hell," Beiste growled. "I've searched half the damned countryside looking for ye. Ye're going to stay right here or I'll lock ye up if I have to."

Erik narrowed his eyes, seemed on the brink of letting out a retort that would have Beiste boxing his ears, but then held his tongue.

"All right. But if ye dinna bring her back, then ye're going to have me to deal with."

Beiste raised his brow and the boy stood taller.

"I might only be a lad now, but one day I'll be a man, Beiste MacDougall, and I've got the blood of leaders running through my veins."

Beiste let out a fierce growl. "Ye'll become the next Irish if ye keep it up."

Erik knew what that meant, knew that Padrig Cam'béal had been at the mercy of the old Laird MacDougall for years before he'd been left on his own. And while his eyes widened for a fraction of a second, then he was smiling.

"An honor. But one day, ye'll see me as much more than that. I swear it." And then he turned on his heel and headed back toward the castle like he owned the place.

Surprisingly, most of Beiste's anger dissipated. Staring after the small form, head held high, Beiste felt a swell of pride.

## 15

*E*lle ran until her lungs were about to burst. She doubled over in the dark forest, hands on her knees, gasping for air. A good hour, or more, had passed with her sprinting as though the ghost of, well, perhaps Bjork himself, were on her tail. Scary thing was, she knew him to be alive and most likely hunting her now. Somehow, she could feel it.

He'd not stop until he had her in his grasp. Wedded, bedded and buried. He'd made that clear when he stormed Castle Gloom and then again when the men who'd come for her at Dunstaffnage had shouted for her return.

Payment for a favor long since erased by the past.

Revenge for what he thought had been stolen from him.

All of it: utter nonsense.

Elle owed Bjork nothing. Until he'd forced his way into her life, she'd only ever heard terrifying accounts of him. Horror tales, but tales all the same. Bjork named himself earl of their family's holdings in Norway. He demanded that all follow him, bow down to him, but Amma refused, and instead helped her own brother to stage a coup, which lost Bjork some of his lands and the loyalty of many. As payment for his loss, Bjork had demanded that her mother marry him, but again, she defied him, sneaking off with the men in a raid. She traveled to Ireland, where she'd met Padrig Cam'béal, and thought to strengthen her brother's power with a marriage alliance. During a raid off the coast of Dunstaffnage with her husband, mother's ship had crashed, and Padrig was taken prisoner. She managed to escape back to Ireland, and held the lands for Padrig while he was imprisoned. (Now, Elle knew that the old Laird MacDougall had set her mother free, and thank goodness, he had.) Meanwhile, back in Norway, Earl Bjork had defeated Amma's brother and claimed all the holdings, including the one in Ireland.

Bjork had fought to get her mother back ever since, constantly raiding—until he'd seen Elle as a girl of perhaps fifteen. Then he'd decided her mother was no longer his prize, but Elle.

Throughout the years, her mother had always assured her he was a long way away. Oh, how wrong she'd been. The man would stop at nothing. Decades of losing had not stopped him. And now, she was certain, he could taste his victory.

Elle closed her eyes a moment, listening to the sounds of the forest, and hoping to catch just the slightest hint of a trickle of water. Her mouth was parched, body covered in slick sweat despite the autumn temperatures. Dizziness licked at the edges of her body. She flexed her hands, having fisted them tightly the entire way. They were tingly, nearly numb. And then she heard it. A slight trickling sound. With one last deep breath, she jogged toward the sound of the burn. She pulled the sword from her back, kneeling before the rushing water to dip her hands in its cool depths. She drank greedily, then scooped up water to splash over her neck and face.

Elle was tired. But she had to keep going. Had to find the bastard. Had to save her brother.

And not be captured by anyone else in the process. That wouldn't do. That would defeat her entire purpose.

Oh, saints, but the water was lovely... She grew lost in the coolness, the way it absorbed into the flesh of her throat. Enough so, she only heard footsteps behind her at the last minute.

"Well...if I believed in ghosts, I might have said you were one."

Elle startled, jumping to her feet. Standing behind her was Bjork, an army of men at his back. He looked much the same. Savage. His hair was sandy in color, streaked with gray at his temples. Scars marred his cheeks, meeting with wrinkles at the corners of his ice-blue eyes. Vacant orbs that flashed with merciless intent when they met hers. His beard was long and woven into a braid that reached near to his chest. His clothes were thick leather, wool and furs, and blood streaked. The sun glinted off his weapons from head to toe. The man was a nightmare. Fierce and evil in his appearance as he was on the inside. She wouldn't be surprised to see that when he smiled, blood from his latest victim dripped from his teeth.

Elle squared her shoulders, willing the trembling of her hands, the knocking of her knees, to quell. She held her head high. "So, ye found me."

"How could I not? You crashed through the forest like a lame bull." His grin widened and he opened his arms wide. "A bull to be sacrificed, and I the altar."

Elle worked hard to return his smile, as though she didn't care about his declarations or the threat that laced them. The imagery of his words was enough to send her into a straight faint, but she somehow managed to remain upright and conscious. "Ye're too generous," she gritted out.

He grunted, greedy eyes scanning over her body with a hunger that sent her blood cold. "I am never generous."

And didn't she know it. "Release my brother. I will surrender myself to ye under those terms."

Confusion flashed on Bjork's face for a fraction of a second. "Your brother?"

"Erik. Release him. Dinna be coy. I know ye have him."

At this, Bjork raised a brow. "I didn't even know you had a brother. Family news doesn't travel fast." He stepped closer to her. "Tell me about this brother."

Elle's chest tightened. Her vision blurred. She was tempted to accuse him of lying, but the steel in his eyes, the firmness of his words…she knew in her heart he was telling the truth. How had no one ever told her Erik was unknown to their enemy? How many other surprises were in store for her?

Elle extended her sword, pointing the tip toward him, her shoulder screaming out with the weight of the heavy weapon.

Bjork raised his brow and chuckled. "As I see it, I've an army and you've none. Even if you swiped at me with that sword, you'd not win. You're in no place to make any negotiations."

Elle swallowed. He had a point, but she refused to let him see that he scared her or that she believed he was right.

"Ye dinna scare me, Bjork."

To that, he laughed all the more, a sound that grated down her spine like the edge of a blade. He slowly walked forward and while she wanted to step back, there was nowhere to go but into the burn. To swim from him. And that was what she did.

~

Beiste tore apart his room—and he knew it was all for naught. The lass had taken the sword, he was certain of it. She'd meet that Viking bastard along the road and he'd not be able to save her.

"Son." Again that same ghostly voice he'd heard when he was bathing in the sea.

Beiste jerked around, completely in denial as to what he was seeing. His father, well, an apparition that *looked* like his father, stood right before him. "Ye're not real."

Beiste stormed toward the door. He had to leave the castle now or else darkness would fall before he could track her steps.

"Son. Ye must go to her."

"What do ye think I'm doing?" Beiste snarled at the vision.

"Making a mess," the ghost said with a shrug and a nonchalant glance around the wrecked chamber.

Beiste's gut wrenched. He missed his father with a passion and here his mind was playing tricks on him. "Why are ye here? To tell me things I already know? To rub the guilt I feel deeper into my soul?"

"Guilt?"

"Aye."

"Guilt for what?" His father gave him the same look he often gave him when he wasn't satisfied with an answer.

"For surviving," Beiste shouted. "For living when everyone else has died."

The ghost of his father waved his hand in the air. "Och, but that is the way of things. The lass, she yet lives. For now."

Beiste narrowed his eyes. If this apparition knew so much, then he was going to demand a few more answers. Worst case scenario—he'd gone completely mad. Best case— he'd get some clarification. "Why does she care so much about that damned sword?"

"I gave it to the Irish." His father shrugged as if it were common knowledge. "It belongs to Erik."

"Erik? Why?"

The ghost looked like he was sighing—if a ghost could breathe. "Erik, is...well, it doesna matter. She went to save him."

"He is here!" Beiste bellowed.

"Mhmm." He nodded. "Fate has played ye both a nasty turn."

"What does that have to do with anything? Ye're wasting my time." Beiste's insides clenched. He had another chance to speak to his father and this was how he was using it? Lord, but he needed to tell him how sorry he was for not being there to protect him. "Apologies, Father. I should have been there for ye. Should have saved ye. And now all this. I am frustrated. I am..."

"Scared."

"Nay!" Bloody hell, warriors didn't get scared!

"'Tis all right to be scared sometimes, lad. But ye're a powerful laird. A good leader. A strong fighter. Ye have heart, even if ye've tried to keep it buried all these years. Go, save her. Bring back the sword and present it to Erik, just as it was supposed to be."

None of this made sense. "Tell me the truth or I let them both go off with the Viking."

The ghost let out a raspy laugh. "Ye'd do no such thing. But I'll tell ye anyway, even though it is not my place. I have sworn an oath. Telling ye will likely mean I'll be punished somehow. Erik, he is—"

The room shook a little, the floorboards trembling beneath Beiste's boots. And then his father was lifted, writhing, and sucked back through a tunnel not of this world, until there was nothing left of him and the room stopped shaking.

"What the bloody hell?" Beiste ran his hands through his hair, unsure if what he'd just witnessed had been a true phenomenon or if he was breaking down. Going completely mad. What he should do is lie down. Rest. He'd not slept in days and now he was hallucinating.

Blast it all. There was no time for sleep. He stormed from the room, back down to the bailey where his men waited. Erik glared at him from the stairs of the keep, staying put as Beiste had ordered him to do.

Beiste leapt onto his horse and, without looking back, ordered his men to gallop through the gates. They were able to easily find Elle's tracks toward the woods. She'd run with no care for anyone following her, which only increased the sense of dread overcoming him. The lass had to be out of her mind.

Anyone could follow her. Animal, outlaw, Viking…the thought was terrifying.

A short time later, they'd made it to the burn where signs of a struggle marred the dirt. That was where the tracks stopped.

"They've crossed the water." Beiste squinted his eyes, studying the ground across the way. There was no sign of anyone, but that didn't mean they'd not been there. "We cross."

They forged into the water, the center growing deeper until the soles of their boots glided over the top. They were lucky that the water had not swelled as much as it normally did with the rainfall they'd had the week before. On the other side, he did, in fact, catch sight of a few tracks, but it appeared that whoever had her—and he was leaning toward Bjork—attempted to cover their steps.

Well, they could try, but they'd not succeed.

Beiste was going to bring her back.

*E*lle breathed hard from her nose, trying not to gag. A dirty rag had been stuffed into her mouth. Her wrists were bound painfully behind her back, but at least her ankles were free. She sat astride a frightfully large warhorse, at Bjork's rear.

Because of her hands being secured behind her, another rope had been tied around her waist and the nasty Viking's, connecting the two of them, entirely too close. He rode hard and her thighs burned from the exertion of trying to hold onto the horse. Despite the rope connecting them, she wobbled all over the place, in danger of falling. The skin at her ribs was rubbed raw from the friction. Her face felt battered from how many times she'd hit it against his spine and shoulder blades. She had no way to brace herself against the speed and rough-ness of their ride. No way to cease the constant agony.

All the while, she kept thinking: what a waste. Offering hers up for naught. And Beiste. Of how he would react when he found her missing. Would he be angry? Relieved? Sad? Delighted?

Her heart lurched to think that he might not even care. That he might whisper, *good riddance*, and never think of her again.

She feared the bond growing between them might have only meant something to her. Been in her head. A grand imagining put there by fairies.

Och, to think that she'd railed at him, that she'd had the audacity to stare him down and think him a failure when she was the one tied to the back of a horse, her brother still nowhere in sight. She'd given herself up to Bjork for no reason. And she'd pay for that foolishness the rest of her days, which she'd determined wouldn't be many.

To say she'd been a fool was to be kind.

This man, who'd killed her family, harmed her people, was now going to take her life. Even if he let her live, she'd be a prisoner. Aye, he wanted to take her to wife, he'd made that perfectly clear when he'd lifted her onto the horse, tying her so tightly to him that her breasts were crushed along the sides of his spine. But, to be his wife, that was a death sentence in itself (as it was, his current wife would be killed so that Elle could replace her, if the woman hadn't been smart enough to run away already).

Nay, Elle would not live. By his hand, her days were numbered.

And then her blood oath would be given to the fairies. Just as they wanted. Perhaps, as they'd planned all along. Mayhap, they'd known her fate and that it wouldn't matter how the oath was met, just that it was.

Elle prayed her eternal life would begin soon. Living with a demonic tormenter was just... She couldn't. Terror ran icy through her veins. There had to be a way to escape. She had to at least try.

The only plus side to her impending death was she'd soon

be able to keep watch over Erik and Beiste, just as the old laird did.

"I… I need to stop," she mumbled around the cloth, but her words came out sounding like, "*Eh… neee tttttt sawwww.*"

No matter, she breathed in deep through her nose and shouted the inaudible words over and over, until Bjork did, finally, call his mount to a halt. But the glower he turned to give her was unmerciful, vicious. He untied their connecting rope and pushed her off the back of the horse. Elle gasped, nearly biting off her tongue when she landed on her arse, a jarring pain shooting up her spine. The men laughed and she managed to crawl to her knees without the use of her hands, then her feet, despite the pain, fearing that she'd mess herself if she didn't find relief soon.

"Go," Bjork said. "Right there."

"Naaayy," she shouted around the gag. She would not debase herself that way. Never would she lift her skirts to relieve herself in front of all these men. Besides, then he would see she still had a weapon, the dagger she'd strapped to her upper thigh. They'd already confiscated the one in her boot. She might be completely despondent but there was still a tiny spark of hope with that steel pressed to her leg.

Bjork nodded to one of his men, not even bothering to take his own future wife to privacy. What did she expect? He'd likely share her with all his men on their wedding night —if not before. Why would he bother to wait for such a thing? She'd try to find a way, any way, to escape before then. Even though she'd promised the old Laird MacDougall she'd never take her own life. She wondered if, in this circum-stance, he would agree.

Lucky for her, the man who escorted her into the trees to relieve herself, cut through the rope at her wrists. He turned his back, grunting for her to get it done. She was surprised at his decency, but hurried to do her business before he decided to emulate his master's crudeness.

Her escort muffled a curse just as she finished, grabbed her by the arm and tied her to a tree. "Stay here."

"What? Where are ye going?" she cried out, wriggling against the ropes.

He jabbed a finger toward her face, his eyes soulless black pools. "Shut your mouth if you want to live."

Elle clamped her mouth shut, not at all disillusioned that he wouldn't take her life and then come up with some excuse to give his master for her demise. She imagined they'd all shrug and then ride off, leaving her bleeding body on the forest floor. Bjork only wanted her because he could torment her. Her life meant nothing to him.

The Viking ran back toward the men. Then she could hear it, the sounds of riders approaching.

And she was tied to a tree…

Saints preserve her! She would not be taken by another horde of whoresons!

Elle wrenched at the ties. He'd not done them as tightly as he could have in his hurry to return to the fray. She wriggled, rubbed, yanked, until they were loosened enough for her to squeeze one hand through. Then she untied her still bound wrist and tossed the rope to the ground. She hiked up her skirt, grabbed her dagger, and prepared to run. To defend herself.

But, what if it was Beiste that had come?

Indecision warred within her. She decided to creep back toward the horses to get a look before she escaped and then her better judgment grasped hold of her. She'd not made it five feet before self-preservation had her turning around. Beiste could handle himself if he met up with Bjork. No need for her interference. She'd only get herself killed. Besides, what if it *wasn't* him?

With that thought in the forefront of her mind, Elle ran in the opposite direction.

Straight into Beiste's arms.

"Beiste!" she shouted, dropping her knife and wrapping her arms around his neck. "How did ye find me?"

He buried his face in her hair, sweeping her up in his arms. Strength and warmth surrounded her. She was certain she'd never been so relieved. "I followed the tracks. And when my scout said Bjork had ye go off into the woods, I separated from my men to head ye off."

"Thank God ye came for me." Her eyes stung with tears. He was so warm. So solid. So strong. Elle pressed her face to his chest and breathed in his familiar scent, trying to wrap her mind around the fact that he was there and the storm of emotions that flooded her entire being.

"I swore to protect ye."

"An oath ye didna have to keep."

Beiste tipped her chin, connecting his gaze with hers. "Aye. I did. I wanted to."

He stared into her eyes and she wanted nothing more than to beg him to kiss her, drown against his lips, his embrace. But the sounds of a battle raged behind them and her heart hammered with fear and trepidation.

"I have to help my men. Come, my horse is over here." He put a hand on her lower back, guiding her to the left. "I want ye to wait for me, hidden. Ride hard if I dinna come back."

"Nay." She jerked to a stop, her gaze searching his. "I want to help."

Beiste looked tired. Shadows darkened beneath his eyes, and his cheeks were stubbled. But he was still the perfect drink of cold water she'd been craving. "Please, Elle, for me. Stay hidden. I have news."

"News?"

"Go. My mount is that way." He whistled and a neighing reply sounded.

Before she could beg him to answer, he was running through the woods, back toward Bjork and his men.

Picking up her knife, Elle made her way the few dozen yards to Beiste's horse, which was also headed toward her. The horse stilled for her to climb onto his broad back and she sat there for perhaps a minute or two before she decided she couldn't simply wait. If there was going to be a battle with Bjork, and Beiste, who she'd enlisted, was going to be a part of it, she couldn't simply sit back and wait. She had to help in any way she could. To prove her own bravery, to show him how much she loved him, how grateful she was.

If only she had the claymore. Damn Bjork for taking the MacDougall legacy.

She felt beneath the saddle blanket and smiled. Just as any true warrior would, Beiste had a second sword stashed there. Withdrawing the blade, she urged his horse to head back toward Bjork. The sounds of battle grew louder the closer she got. Shouts, clangs, cries.

By the time she broke through the trees, many of the Vikings lay on the ground and so did a few of the Scots. The rest were in hard combat. Slicing, blocking, hacking. Shouts of anger, bellows of pain. It left her speechless with fear and angst. She stared through the throngs of fighting men searching for Beiste and Bjork. Why she didn't spot them right away through the various blurs of tartan and leather was a mystery.

They two were the largest of men. The fiercest. The most angry. Each of them was splattered with blood, teeth barred. Their weapons clashed so hard together sparks flew from the sharp edges of their weapons.

Her grip faltered on the sword. Thinking she could somehow aide in this fight had been a mistake. Why couldn't she stick with her original plan of running? Of letting Beiste handle Bjork on his own? Why did she have to be so stupid?

Aye, she'd practiced fencing at Castle Gloom, but never had she been in a true battle. If she were to get in Beiste's way, he could be harmed. The horse sensed her agitation, worry, and instead of backing up as she commanded, the animal surged forward into the fray.

Elle let out an ear-piercing scream, grappling with the reins, trying to pull back as hard as she could, but it was hard with a massive sword in one hand. And she didn't want to drop it. As it was, men took the opportunity to rush her and she swiped one away with the sword. She was grateful to Gunnar who grappled another. Even her horse got in on the action, rising up on his hind legs and bopping a man with his thick head and forelegs.

Beiste caught sight of her, momentarily distracted. She screamed as Bjork raised his sword, prepared to levy a death stroke on her beloved.

Aye, she loved him. Intensely.

"Beiste! Watch out!"

He turned in time, raising his claymore to block the blow. Seeing her seemed to give him a renewed sense of strength, a supernatural power. He intensified his assault, tackling Bjork to the ground with a piercing battle cry. All around her, men fought to the death. One by one, the Vikings fell, either dead or too injured to continue. Beiste's men seemed to possess a sense of honor, not bothering with killing off the wounded, but taking down those who continued to fight.

Gaze fastened on Beiste, fear pummeling her insides, Elle watched him crush Bjork beneath his fists. He used no weapons. He continued to pound away until the man who'd killed her parents, killed Beiste's father, no longer breathed, his face a mush of blood and bone. With his death, her torment should have ended, but she continued to feel the heavy burden of so much loss. An ache she suspected would take some time to heal.

As soon as Beiste stood, his eyes turned toward her. She felt dizzy with relief, affection, and something so strong, she couldn't even name it.

He charged toward her, nearly ripping her from the horse, his mouth claiming hers for all to see.

Elle clung to him, arms around his neck, body pressed tightly to his, she wished they were one. That she'd never leave his side, that they could be together forever.

"I didna think..." She started peppering his face with kisses and he threaded his hands in her hair and breathed her in. "God, I was terrified. If he'd have..." She couldn't even say the word *killed*, it was too painful to contemplate.

"Ye should have remained hidden," he growled, his fingers digging into her back as he crushed his mouth to hers again. "Ye should have listened. Ye could have been killed." He spoke between kisses, leaving her breathless and speechless all at once.

"I couldna. I... I needed to help. Needed to see that ye lived! I love ye. Did ye hear me? I *love ye!*" Love! She'd confessed to him her feelings, split open her heart and shared it.

At her words, Beiste pushed her to arm's length, dark clouds storming in his eyes. He shook his head. Didn't say anything.

She waited, heart wide open, tears stinging her eyes as he denied her feelings with that subtle shake of his head.

"Ye shouldna." Then he turned his back and walked away.

## 17

The ride back to Dunstaffnage Castle was arduous, and painstakingly long given they were only a few miles away. Every pound of his mount's hoof echoed in Beiste's mind.

They'd won the battle, crushed their enemies, saved the woman with nary a scratch—and he'd never felt more horrible and defeated in his life.

At least Beiste had cleaned the gore of battle from his skin by the river. The only blood on his person now was the invisible blood of the woman's heart he'd broken—and that of his own shredded soul.

Elle sat pillion on his horse, her arms encircling his waist, her breasts to his back, her face pressed to his spine. She clung to him and though it was mostly because they were riding hard back to the castle, he also hoped it was because she *needed* him.

Och, but, nay! How could he want such a thing? He had no right to want it, let alone wish it. Especially after her confession, how he'd smashed her offer, her gift of love as though he were the worst kind of monster alive. A true beast.

She *loved* him?

Beiste tried to grapple with that admission. *Love. Love. Love.*

What was love?

What did it mean?

Did he deserve it?

Could he return it?

Would it be the death of her?

Lord, help him, but he already knew he loved her. With every fiber of his being. His heart sung to hear her words, his body had literally tingled. And then his mind had laid a cracking whip against his chest, laying him open, exposed and wounded.

Everyone he loved perished. *Died.* Did he really want that for her? Was it too late for her, because he loved her so deeply? Was she already doomed to a terrible fate? Or had she now escaped that fate right before his eyes? Hell, he'd just battled the very devil himself who'd taken her—and she was still living and breathing. They had *won.* She was not dead, but alive and breathing behind him.

Thriving.

Was it possible, truly, that whatever terrible curse he'd been punished with had been lifted?

Beiste glanced down at her hands pressed to his middle, his own arm holding on to those precious limbs. She'd think that he simply held on to her for practicality's sake, but it wasn't. He liked touching her. Wanted to touch her. Didn't know what the bloody hell he was going to do about it. Couldn't even contemplate what it would be like to go through the rest of his life not touching her, seeing her smile, hearing her voice.

Was that what Beiste's father was trying to tell him when he sent him after her? What had his father wanted to tell him before he'd been sucked back into Purgatory? Or wherever he was...

There was a storm of questions and worry plunging around inside him. Planning and executing a battle was easier than figuring out what to do about the woman he loved. If she'd even have him after such a rejection.

The ride back to the castle only took an hour. As soon as they were through the gates, he helped Elle down from her horse. Her waist was warm and tiny in his hands. 'Twas hard not to bury his face in her hair. He settled for breathing in the floral, comforting scent of her, for grazing his lips ever so gently across her temple. She avoided his gaze; her eyes focused somewhere near their feet.

Beiste licked his lower lip, prepared to speak. The words teetering on the tip of his tongue. *I love ye, too.* But he couldn't risk it. Who was to say if her not being harmed wasn't just a coincidence? How could he risk her life for his own selfish reasons?

Blast it all, he couldn't live with her, but he couldn't live without her either.

"Elle—" he started, but was cut off by young Erik calling out to his sister at the same time.

Her eyes widened, her mouth fell open, and the color drained from her face. "Erik?" she whispered, then squeezed her eyes shut, murmuring something about a ghost.

Had his father been to see her, too? Beiste wanted to ask but instead took a step back to allow for their reunion.

Erik threw himself against his sister, knocking her off balance. Beiste steadied them both, feeling his chest swell with emotion.

"Surprise," Beiste said. "Your brother."

Elle wrapped her arms around Erik. "Why did ye not tell me?" she asked. Then shook her head. "Never mind. I'm just glad he's safe." She kissed the lad's head. "Ye're not harmed? Bjork did not hurt ye?"

"He never found me." Erik beamed. "I presented myself to Laird MacDougall on Ben Vorlich and returned to Dunstaffnage upon his insistence. Had I known ye were here…"

"Never mind that," she said. "We'll not speak of regrets when there is so much to celebrate."

"Aye, sister, we have survived." The triumphant look on the lad's face was heartwarming.

"Aye. Against all odds. Where are Glenna, Barra and Mary?"

"We were separated in the woods when the Vikings came through. When they ran one way, I ran another. I didna want them to find me, because I knew I would only endanger them more."

"I'm so glad ye're safe." Elle hugged him close to her again, then she glanced up at Beiste, regret shining in the depths of her face. "We'll soon be on our way, my laird. I thank ye from the bottom of my heart for your help. I hope one day, I can repay ye."

Beiste shook his head, deciding then and there he wasn't going to ask about the sword. Perhaps that was a mystery that he'd never get solved. He'd recovered the sword from Bjork's dead body, who must have taken it from Elle. It belonged to Erik. His father had gifted the weapon to him in the first place. He handed her the claymore. "This belongs to ye." Elle's eyes widened and she glanced briefly at her brother as she grasped the jeweled hilt. "There is no need to repay me, my lady. Ye have no debt with me. Ye owe me nothing. 'Tis my duty," he murmured, sensing how utterly distant and heartless he sounded considering her earlier admission of love.

Elle's eyes burned into his and he could only imagine the

many things she was saying in her mind. *Coward,* being one of them.

He couldn't look at her anymore. For that was what he was. A coward. But wasn't her life worth him running? How could he push on her the curse that seemed to rule him from the day he was born? Beiste bowed his head and, once more, turned his back on her.

His feet were heavy as he walked away. His body rigid. It felt like every single inch of him was trying to remain rooted in place as he pulled away. Separating his body from his soul. His soul remaining with her. He knew he'd never be the same again. Lost, cold, soulless. An empty shell of a man.

Damn, but he'd not realized how much he loved her. Needed her. Wanted her.

The two dozen steps from her to the keep stairs were the longest and most painful he'd ever taken in his life.

This couldn't be right. It couldn't.

He paused. One foot on the stair. There was an unfamiliar sting in his eyes. He ran a hand through his hair, trying to grapple with the turmoil and then he felt her hand on his arm.

"Beiste. Before ye walk away," she said, softly, her green eyes mirroring his pain. "There is something ye need to know."

Pulling in a shuddering breath, he turned to face her fully. Her dark red hair was wild, her cheeks still pink from the excitement of seeing her brother. Though the gown she wore was torn and dirty, he'd never seen her look more radiant.

"What is it?" he said softly.

Elle was beautiful, devastatingly so. Her arm was slung protectively over her brother's shoulders.

"Erik, he is not my brother by blood."

Beiste glanced between the two of them, seeing very little

resemblance, but not grasping just what she meant. "I dinna understand."

"Erik is *your* brother."

Beiste's throat tightened. When he looked at the lad and thought him familiar, now he knew why. His eyes were the same blue as their father's. The stubborn tilt of his chin was the same as his own. Family—his blood. A brother. As impossible as it seemed, he could see the familiarly in the young lad's visage. Was this what his father had been trying to tell him?

"How?"

Elle tugged Erik forward a step. "Can we talk inside?"

Beiste glanced at the men around the courtyard, taking care of the horses, their weapons, drinking from the well. No one seemed to take note at all that such life-altering news had been laid upon him. "Aye," he said, a little breathless. This news changed so much. The curse, it would seem, had been a figment of his imagination, or a terrible coincidence.

"Erik," she said. "Go and get something to eat from the kitchens. Lord knows ye need it."

Dutifully, the lad nodded and trotted away.

Elle slid her warm hand in Beiste's, the delicate skin of her palms rubbing against his rougher hand. "Shall we?"

Beiste stared down at their fingers entwined, and thanked every saint he could think of that Elle ignored his beastly rejection, because right now, he knew one thing—he was never letting her go.

## 18

Though she was still feeling devastated that her love was shoved aside by Beiste, at least Elle could give him this parting gift. A sibling. Something he'd been saying since they met that he had always desperately wanted. Not to be alone. Not to be the last.

The news she'd given him had been shocking, and that was evident by the paleness of his face, but also seemed to have bolstered him. He threaded his fingers with hers and squeezed. She clutched back, trying to offer him comfort and strength and love, even if he wouldn't accept it. Soon enough, she'd be gone from his life.

She'd return to Castle Gloom and try to put it back together, until Beiste sent Erik there to rule. She assumed he'd want his brother here, to get to know one another to make up for the time they'd lost. So, he could train his brother, protect him. Lord, but she'd miss having Erik around. She'd been just a lass when he was born and so many years she'd spent helping to raise him, protect him.

Beiste seemed to shake himself from his shock and led her through the castle to his study, shutting the door behind them both. This was a room she'd yet to explore. The walls were lined with bookshelves, save for the places reserved for two arrow-slit windows, a doorway toward an antechamber, and a wide hearth. The shelves were filled with texts and scrolls. A long trestle table was covered with more scrolls and maps. His desk was much the same way, piled high with parchment and record books. The idea of him working in organized chaos made her smile.

He moved to the desk, which housed a jug of whisky and a few cups, and poured himself a healthy dram of whisky, offering her one.

Elle shook her head. She needed all her wits about her. Every shred would be used in resisting the urge to demand he tell her why he couldn't admit to his feelings. Why he pushed her away.

He brought the cup to his lips and sipped slowly, instead of throwing it back like she thought he might. In fact, given how intoxicated he'd been the night she first met him, she expected him to simply drink from the bottle. But she'd gotten to know him over the last couple of weeks, and there was one thing Beiste wasn't and that was irresponsible. 'Twas one thing to drown his sorrows, and quite another to give himself a nip of liquid courage.

Elle let out a deep sigh. She had to get this over with. And leave. Because all she kept thinking about was how handsome he was. How much she loved him and wanted to kiss him. What it would be like to live out her days with him. To convince him that they were right for each other.

Elle cleared her throat and paced to the far wall, tracing her fingers over several texts. Erik would adore the sheer number of volumes. "When my father, Padrig, was here, he and your father became close confidants. Despite the fact that he'd once been found raiding on your lands and your father took him prisoner." Elle laughed, recalling her boisterous father and wondering how he'd ever humbled himself to the MacDougall. "Then he eventually was made an indentured servant. Padrig watched as your mother lost bairn after bairn. Then one night, while your mother was taking a walk to ease her labor pains that she'd kept hidden, she fell down in the gardens, unable to move, her labor starting in earnest. My father happened to be fixing part of the wall and stopped to see if she was all right." Flicking her gaze toward him, she saw that Beiste kept his gaze steady on hers not revealing any of his thoughts on his face. She continued, wanting the truth to be set free. The quicker she got it done, the quicker she'd be on her way. "She grabbed hold of his arm and begged him to help her, telling him that the bairn was coming quick. Nervous, but unable to do anything but help, my father found Erik was, indeed, nearly born. The head was delivered, shoulders, and the rest of his body soon slithered out onto the garden floor." Elle paused, checking Beiste's features, trying to gauge his reaction.

He was stunned, rigid. His lips clamped. The cup of whisky in his hand forgotten.

"Father picked him up, wrapping him in the extra length of his plaid. Erik looked right up into his eyes and let out a healthy wail. Not something the previous bairns had the strength to summon. Your mother begged him to take the bairn away. To raise him away from the curse of the castle."

"My curse," Beiste growled.

Elle shook her head. "Nay. Ye were not the first born to them. Your parents thought when ye survived ye were the breaker of curses. They tried for more children, but it seemed ye were a gift, and then Erik, too."

"There were others before me? No one ever told me…"

"Perhaps they did not want to burden ye with such sadness."

He nodded, his jaw tight. "And Erik was raised all this time without my knowing."

"Aye." She licked her lips. "Your father agreed with your mother's wishes and gifted Padrig, my father, Castle Gloom. My mother and I were summoned from Ireland to live with my father. Though he is not my blood, he's always been my brother. We loved him as though he were one of us."

Beiste scrubbed a hand over his face. "Ye were not here before, in Scotland? Why?"

Elle shook her head. "My father had come over to Scotland during a raid and never returned. Mother had long thought him dead. She gave birth to me just before he left. Gone for ten long years before she had a word. My mother fought all those years to keep herself in my father's homeland. Bjork believed her to be a traitor, that she was owed to him as a wife, and then subsequently myself."

Beiste briefly touched her face, emotions she couldn't comprehend showing in his eyes. "Thank God that bastard is gone from your life." He blew out a heavy breath, his hand falling. "Saints, but I have a brother."

Elle laughed softly. "Aye."

"And that is why my father gave Erik the sword. Why he pledged to protect your clan."

"Mhmm. So he'd know it was the truth should something ever happen to him. But more importantly, so ye would believe."

Beiste scrubbed his hands over his face. "Ye have given me a great gift."

Elle's throat tightened so much that she couldn't speak. But she summoned the strength to whisper. "I'd have given ye more."

Beiste's face contorted slightly, pinching, as though he held back a flood of emotion. "I've been a fool. A terrible beast."

Elle smoothed out her skirts, wanting to back away. To run. Now was a good time, before her heart broke even further.

"I threw away the other precious gift ye gave me. Even when I wanted it. I didna think I deserved it. Didna think if I accepted it that I could keep ye safe from my curse."

"What gift?" she asked, tears stinging her eyes. It couldn't be what she hoped it was. She tried to keep the shield up around her heart, to deflect the pain. But it wasn't working.

"Love."

Oh, zounds! Her heart pounded, near to exploding. She clutched at the shelf, hoping it would steady her. "Ye canna throw away a person's feelings. They are still here, right out in the open. All ye have to do is accept them."

He marched toward her, covering the ground between them in a few strides. "I want to. I do." Beiste clutched her up in his arms, holding her tight. "I love ye, lass. With all my heart and soul and being. I feared for ye. Feared that if I loved ye, if I accepted your love in return, that something would happen to ye. 'Tis why I so foolishly pushed ye away."

Tears were streaming from her eyes now, and she was powerless to stop them. Her hands trembled. Knees knocked together. "My destiny is already sealed. And so is yours."

"What destiny is that?" His voice was whisper soft as he gazed into her eyes and tenderly wiped her tears away.

Elle dared not tell him about becoming a *glaistig*. She knew that if she did, he would reject her fully, hoping that by doing so he'd spare her eternal life. But his rejection would do nothing, for Fate had already chosen.

So, instead, she said, "That we two should be together. It was meant to be."

"Aye." He smoothed a thumb over her cheek. "I love ye. I want ye to be my wife. Will ye do me the honor of marrying this fool? This beast?"

"Nay. I will not marry a fool or a beast." She smiled and tickled his ribs. "But I will marry *ye*, Beiste MacDougall, the most kind, daring and resilient man I know."

And then he kissed her hard, both of their emotions spilling out into that meeting of mouths. Their bodies clashed together and when he swept her up into his arms, carrying her through his study and into a bedchamber, Elle didn't stop him. This was her love. This was the man she'd spend the rest of her life with. A man she'd create children with.

And then she knew. Her fate as the *glaistig* was not a curse —but a blessing, because she'd be able to watch over her children, her grandchildren, and every generation to come. *Her* people. *Her* blood. Beiste's blood. *Their* blood.

Beiste disrobed her slowly, kissing every inch of her skin, memorizing every plane, caressed along the rope burn at her ribs, and then rose to touch his lips to hers. She removed his clothing, studying the hard ridges and dips of his contoured body, running her hands over the scars he'd received in battles past.

"Saints, my love, but ye are beautiful," he murmured, caressing the outline of her naked form.

"And so are ye."

"I've never been called such before," he chuckled.

"They are all fools who dinna see it." She reached for him, relishing the weighty feel of his body against hers, pressing her firmly into the mattress, all hard lines against her softer flesh.

"Perhaps we should wait," Beiste said, sliding kisses over her shoulders and down to the valley between her breasts.

Elle sucked in a ragged breath, her body on fire, her mind whirling. "Perhaps. But why wait for our future when we can seize it right now?"

ELIZA KNIGHT

The man she loved gazed deeply into her eyes. "Och, love, ye have stolen my heart."

She smiled, reached up to graze her fingertips over his stubbled cheeks. "And ye have stolen mine."

Beiste kissed her then, making her heart soar, her blood pummel with excitement through her veins. Every inch of her reached out to him, tugging him closer. She clung to his back, his muscles thick and rippling beneath her fingertips. She wrapped her legs around his hips, feeling the hardness of his arousal press against the apex of her thighs. Frissons of startling pleasure coursed through her at the contact. Love so deep and swirling consumed her. Ignited her passion.

Elle wanted more. All of him. A month ago, as she argued the merits of becoming a wife, she never would have guessed that she'd be here in this man's arms. Trustingly. Willingly. Lovingly.

Beiste ran his hands over her abdomen and down to her mound, sliding between the slickened folds. "Ye're ready for me, love."

Elle sucked in a heady breath. "Aye, please, dinna make me wait."

"But *I* am not ready for *ye*," he teased.

She pouted, feeling the very rigid, hard shaft. "How?"

There was a wicked glint in his eyes. "I want to see ye find pleasure first. I want to *taste* every inch of ye."

"What?" This had her confused.

Beiste winked as he lowered his lips to the valley between her breasts, and kissed his way down her body, his shoulders pushing her thighs wide, his hands pressing to her inner thighs, exposing her sex more to his view.

"Beiste...," she said uneasily.

"This, my love. This." He flicked his tongue over her core and Elle's head fell back, a moan rushing from her throat. "This is what I want."

"Aye, that..." Heaven help her, this was wicked and wonderful all at once.

He made love to her with his mouth, sending her mind and body into a tailspin of pleasure. She soared, riding higher and higher with every kiss, lick and nuzzle. Until she felt herself shatter through and through, crying out with the intensity of the sensations racking her.

Beiste smiled, looming over her, pressing his length once more against her. He surged forward, breaking the barrier of her maidenhead. There was a pinch of pain, but she hardly felt it, her mind still reeling from what he'd done with his tongue.

Before she could even grasp the pure delight of their union, he was moving within her. Kissing her neck, her lips. Stroking her hair. Telling her just how beautiful she was and that he could not live without her. That she'd changed him. Saved him. Taken away the darkness.

Elle clung to him, told him how much of a gift he was to her. That she'd not thought love was possible, only to finally find him. That he completed her. Made her look forward to each day and every new adventure.

And she meant it. She was going to cherish each and every day she had with him. Every moment of this life. Because her memories, her time with him, would help to get her through an eternity of walking the earth.

"I love ye, Beiste," she whispered against his ear, growing bold, and tickling his earlobe with her tongue.

He growled in response, scraping his teeth along her neck providing her with a wicked shiver. "I love ye, too, lass."

"Now and forever."

"Always."

"I dreamt of ye once, and do ye know what ye said?"

"That I canna live without ye?"

Elle giggled, and repeated the words that had comforted

her many a night. "For a beast, I am aptly named. And by no lass shall I be tamed, save for the one whose stolen my soul, the only one to make me whole."

"Saints, preserve me, but 'tis true."

And then the time for talking was over, as they melted into one another and the pleasure of their bodies, their love, and of this moment that led them toward the next.

A life away from shadow. A strength to take on their enemies. A will to live life to the fullest. A love that would last an eternity.

# EPILOGUE

*B*eiste paced the great hall, the sounds of his wife's labor echoing through his head more than the actual castle walls. Many of the clan waited anxiously. Even Glenna, Barra and Mary had come for the birth of the MacDougall heir. The entire territory was rampant with anticipation.

He imagined everything that could go wrong, going wrong. The bairn wouldn't be turned the right way. Maybe it would be too big. Maybe Elle didn't have the strength—nay this last one made no sense.

Elle had proven to him time and again that she was the strongest woman he was ever to know.

Bravest.

Smartest.

Most beautiful.

Most humorous.

Aye, she was perfect in every way. Even her stubborn streak amused him.

And so, he could not lose her. Not to childbirth.

He paused at the hearth, pressing his hands to the mantel and hung his head, working through his emotions, his fear.

"My laird." Gunnar handed him a pewter mug filled with strong whisky.

"Thank ye." Beiste gulped it in one swallow.

"I needed a few drams when my wife was birthing." Gunnar gave him a knowing nod.

"Does the fear ever leave?" He glanced up at the rafters, imagining his wife's struggle, wishing he could take on the pain for her.

Gunnar shook his head. "I'd like to tell ye it does, but it willna. Even after the bairn is born, then ye've got a whole host of things to worry over."

Beiste groaned and Gunnar gave him a refill. He tipped the cup back, letting the whisky burn its path to his belly.

"Another?"

"Aye."

Gunnar refilled his cup once more, then filled one for himself, raising it in the air. "May the road rise up to meet ye. May the wind be always at your back. May the sun shine warm upon your face. The rains fall soft upon your fields and until we meet again, my friend, may God hold ye in the palm of His hand."

"*Sláinte*."

Gunnar did a good job at keeping Beiste distracted, until his laird could finally stand it no longer, and tore his way up the castle stairs in search of his wife.

He came upon their chamber just as the door opened and one of the maids stepped out.

"Ye've arrived just in time to meet your son, my laird."

"My son..." Beiste felt all the air whoosh from his chest, then fill up once more with pride. "I have a son."

"Aye."

He glanced at the door, itching to push through. "And my wife?"

The maid smiled and nodded. "Lady Elle is doing verra well."

Beiste didn't wait to hear anything further. He swept into the room, taking in the sight of his wife, hair dark and slickened with sweat. Her skin was pale, but her eyes bright. Perspiration soaked her chemise, and the sheets beneath her were reddened and being swept away by the ladies who'd attended her.

But despite the scariness of those sights, in her arms she held a bundle of squirming pink, and a smile filled her face, pure joy. She'd never looked more beautiful to him.

"Beiste, come look," she said, waving him closer.

He sat on the side of the bed, gazing down at his son, dark curls on his head.

"He is beautiful," Beiste murmured.

She smiled, stroking their bairn's plump cheek. "He is perfect."

"Thank ye, my love, for giving me so many precious gifts." He stroked his hand over the soft downy head of his son and gazed into Elle's eyes.

"Nothing has ever made me happier."

"Oh, my love." Beiste kissed her gently, smoothing the hair away from her face. Their son gave a little gurgle that drew their attention back. "What shall we call him?"

Elle seemed to have already made a choice, as she did not hesitate to answer. "Torquil, after your father."

Beiste chuckled. "I was going to say Padrig, after yours."

"Then we shall call him, Torquil Padrig MacDougall."

"A more noble name there never was." Beiste kissed his precious son on the forehead then kissed his wife, his love, his everything.

## THE END

*If you enjoyed* **LAIRD OF SHADOWS**, *please spread the word by leaving a review on the site where you purchased your copy, or a reader site such as Goodreads or Shelfari! I love to hear from readers, too, so drop me a line at* authorelizaknight@gmail.com *OR visit me on Facebook:* https://www.facebook.com/elizaknightauthor. I'm also on Twitter: @ElizaKnight. If you'd like to receive my occasional newsletter, please sign up at www.elizaknight.com. *Many thanks!*

There are more books in the MacDougall Legacy! Keep reading for an excerpt of *Laird of Twilight*!

*A future foretold...*
*Only one man can fulfill her destiny...*

Lady Lilias Cameron has spent the last thirteen years skeptical of a prophecy regarding her future—until the very man described by the seer is introduced as her escort to a doomed marriage. Brooding and handsome, she cannot help the sparks of awareness he triggers. Nor can she ignore the deep desire to be true to herself.

Dirk MacDougall, Lord of the Isles, is to deliver a worthy bride to his Norse enemy, in an alliance that will hopefully bring peace to his country. The only problem is, he finds himself quite enamored by the spirited and charming lady. When one kiss leads to another, desire to claim her as his own takes hold.

If the alliance is broken, a mighty battle will be waged across Scotland begging the question: is forbidden love worth the price of war?

PROLOGUE

*Scottish Highlands*
   *Year of Our Lord, 1251*

WITHOUT A DOUBT, THIS WAS THE SCARIEST DAY OF LILIAS CAMERON'S LIFE.

Twilight crept over the forest, sneaking up on Lilias and her lady mother at a pace neither had anticipated. As if the wood sought the darkness, craved it. They came to a clearing ringed by trees that looked to have taken wide steps away from a small, dilapidated croft at the center. For certes, it was the spookiest of places wee Lilias had ever seen.

The wattle and daub croft was dark, no candle or firelight cast from the single window, or the cracks in the weathered door. No smoke curled from the chimney. Growing up the sides were twisted vines that seemed to reach for the sky, pushing past the sagging limbs of the overbearing trees that hovered above the roof. The croft was not in the least welcoming. It lacked life. For as much as she could tell, there was no one about at all.

"Mama, I dinna like this place," Lilias said, with a shiver.

"We'll not be long, Lili." Her mother's fingers held firm to her arm, correctly suspecting Lilias's desire to run—and she would, if given the chance.

At just shy of seven summers, her vivid imagination was running wild at what manner of creatures the eerie croft and woods at dusk possessed.

"Why are we here?" Her voice came out so low, she was surprised her mother heard her at all.

"I've explained already." Mama dragged her closer to the door. Suspicious in the extreme, Lady Cameron had been having dreams lately of her daughter in trouble. What exactly those dreams contained, Lilias didn't know for certain. She'd only heard her mother lament of them to her father. Whenever Lilias drew near enough to eavesdrop, her mother always seemed to sense she was in the vicinity. The awareness her mother had when it came to Lilias was almost magical in its power to reveal her at every turn. Enough so that Lilias often wondered if her mother weren't a magical creature herself.

If that were the case, then she could keep Lilias safe now, couldn't she?

As they approached the door, the wind howled and the leaves rustled. Rubbing together in a way that sounded like a hundred tiny footsteps danced all around them. If she squeezed her eyes shut tight enough, she could see the glowing sprites grinning as they whirled.

Lilias bit the inside of her cheek to keep from whimpering in fear, and she scooted closer to her mother, grateful now for the firm grip on her arm.

Though it was summer, when the sun had set this evening, a chill swept over the moors. They wore their cloaks, but even the thick wool didn't keep the brisk air from sweeping up the hem of her gown, and the invisible icy hands scraping over her hose.

"I'm scared," Lilias said.

Mama glanced down at Lilias, her eyes shining from where the moon crept through the branches overhead. "Hush, now, Lili. Dinna be afraid. We are here to see what the future holds."

With her knuckles, Mama gave two swift knocks and then three more. It sounded like a pattern, a code. Mama held her breath and Lilias counted to seven. Mother did the same sequence of knocking once more, and then seven breaths later, the door burst open.

If possible, the chill from the air that whooshed from within was colder than the temperature outside.

Lilias shuddered once more, gooseflesh rising on every part of her body as she stared into the void. There was no one standing beyond the threshold, just blackness and the scent of musty herbs. Who had opened the door? A ghost? Something far worse?

"Mama…" Lilias sought her mother's hand and wound their fingers, clutching tight and not caring about the hard metal of her mother's rings that bit into the sensitive flesh of her fingers.

Mama glanced down, love and hope shining in her eyes. "All will be well. Ye need only reach inside yourself, love. Ye alone have the strength to endure." Mama straightened her shoulders, her jaw thrusting forward with determination, and she tugged Lilias inside.

As soon as they were across the threshold, the door

swung shut behind them, followed by a loud click as the handle latched and locked. The echoes of the rustling leaves, the howling wind, it all dissipated in that one moment, leaving them in complete silence. And darkness.

She couldn't see anything, as though they'd slipped into a black void. If not for her mother's hold, Lilias would have bolted. She opened her mouth to tell her mother, once more, of her fear, but the grip on her arm lightened, mama's signal that she was…relaxing? If her mother wasn't afraid, then why should she be? Suddenly, Lilias did feel stronger. What her mother said was true—she could endure.

"I have been expecting ye." An old woman's voice scratched from somewhere to their right.

There was the sound of a flint-rock being struck and then light came from a single candle illuminated the room from a rickety, round wooden table. Herbs hung from the rafters of the croft, explaining the smell. The dim candlelight cast large and odd-shaped shadows over the floor and walls. Sitting in a chair by the hearth was an old crone with silver hair that danced in the candlelight. Shoulders stooped, long chin reaching close to her chest, hooked nose mottled with bumps, she looked as though she'd lived to be one hundred twenty years.

How had she lit the candle from the chair? There was at least six feet between the two. And there was no way the old woman had been able to get from the table to the chair without them having seen. Or quickly for that matter. She looked as though she'd not left the chair in a very long time.

"Magic," the old crone whispered.

Lilias glanced up at her mother, certain she'd not spoken her question aloud. The crone had read her thoughts. There was a word on the tip of Lilias's mind—*witch*—that she dared not speak aloud.

The older woman clucked her tongue, disapproving of

this thought. "I am a seer. A *taibhsear*, not a witch, ye ken? Come closer, child. Stand before me. Let us not dally.

When Lilias made no move to go forward, Mama tugged her closer to the empty hearth, her numb feet begrudgingly sliding over the earthen floor.

The musty, herbal scent grew as they approached the *taibhsear*, as though it were the seer's own essence that permeated the single room, and not the dried bundles.

"Ye have come seeking answers about your daughter's future?" Rather than look at mother at all, the seer kept her steady, hard gaze on Lilias.

"Aye." Lady Cameron's voice was strong. Nevertheless, Lilias could sense the underlying fear, and she hoped that her mother's anxiety stemmed only from what she was going to learn and not the *taibhsear* herself.

"Closer, child."

Lilias took tentative steps forward, her mother's pointy fingers in the small of her back urging her on. When her boots touched the tips of the seer's, she stopped. She couldn't look the old woman in the eyes. They were so dark, so deep, seeming to reach the ends of the earth.

The *taibhsear* leaned forward, her bones creaking. She grabbed hold of Lilias's hand, her fingers sharp with bone. Turning over the palm, she ran a crooked nail over the center of Lilias's palm. A chill darted through Lilias and she tried to clench her fingers closed, to hide her palm from the woman's view, but some unseen force kept her fingers open.

"She has an important destiny." The seer dragged out the last word in long, breathy syllables.

Mama shifted beside Lilias, her body stiffening. "I can only pray 'tis so."

Her grip on Lilias's hand tightened. "Did ye bring payment?"

"Aye." Mama pressed a ruby ring into the crone's gnarled hand.

The *taibhsear* slipped the ring onto her own finger as though it were a perfect fit, and then reached up, hands steady when they looked like they should be shaking.

The seer touched Lilias's forehead, the cold, bony tips of her fingers chilling Lilias's skin to a sting. "I see… a man who commands twilight."

Mother gasped. "Is he coming for her?"

"Shh…" The seer rebuked, one eye popping open in disproval as she eyed Mama, then slammed it closed once more. Her lips pursed and she hummed. "Summer shall come to pass thirteen times before he makes his presence known."

"Who *is* he?" Mama asked impatiently, and Lilias too wondered at this stranger who was going to get her. She imagined a demon rising from the earth. Crawling toward her, reaching, and dragging her to his deep, dark, desolate lair.

"He is dark of hair, stormy of eye, and fiercer than the wickedest gale storm. This laird of twilight shall wed Lilias."

*Nay!* She did not *want* to wed, and especially not a man as terrifying as this one sounded.

The devil himself may be her future husband.

"So, she will live at least that long." Mama blew out a breath of relief. "In my dreams—"

The seer's eyes flew open, meeting with Mama's. She removed her hand from Lilias's forehead and placed it over Lady Cameron's face. "Those dreams… they are not about your daughter."

"Then who?"

The seer shook her head, removed her hand, and took a step backward. "I dinna know."

"How can ye not know?" Frustration oozed from every one of Mama's words.

"I am drained." The *taibhsear* sank back into her chair, as though the effort to sit up was too much now.

"Ye want more? I can give ye…" Her mother grabbed for another ring on her finger, but the seer stopped her with a shake of her head.

"No more today, my lady. Ye wanted to know your daughter's future, and I have given it to ye." She closed her eyes and slowly traced something in the air. "A man who commands twilight. Dark of hair. Stormy of eye. Fiercer than the wickedest gale storm. He is her future. Her destiny was written in the stars many years ago. There is nothing that can be done to change it."

Lilias frowned as the candle on the table flickered, and Mama ushered her from the quickly darkening croft. Outside, the door slammed closed once more, all life from within seeming to be extinguished.

Lilias did not want a man to be her future. She wanted to forge her own path. But saying such to her mother was out of the question. No doubt now, and until this laird of twilight made himself known, Mama would search out every warrior with a stormy look to his eyes.

Well, Lilias would keep her eyes steady, too. But she'd be looking out for the demon husband who wished to claim her, if only to plan her escape.

CHAPTER ONE

～

*Winter, 1262*
*Near Dunstaffnage*

IF DIRK HAD TO STARE ACROSS A FIELD OF BATTLE AND see his cousin's face again, he was going to make certain the man finally made it to his grave. As it was, he was currently hacking through a force of Morten Olafsson's men and couldn't rightly shout that to the blasted man. No matter that the blood of their ancestors ran through both their veins: Olafsson was his to vanquish. The sooner, the better, for Dirk was growing mighty tired of having his cousin marching on his moor and demanding surrender.

Sometime past dawn, a scout had slammed his fists on the great doors of Dunstaffnage Castle, warning Dirk of the impending attack. *Again.*

Dirk's power-hungry, land-stealing, pillaging-and-plundering *very* distant cousin, Morten Olafsson, just wouldn't cease.

This was the fifth time in as many months Dirk had to call his men to arms. This time, though, rather than allowing his cousin to come to the castle walls where Dirk soundly beat him, he'd decided it was a good idea to bring the battle to Olafsson. His cousin was under the inferior belief that he was the mightier of the two because he made it to Dirk's walls the last four times—though he'd yet to breach them. And that was the reason he continued to bring on the fight, though he'd yet to win.

Well, no more.

This came to an end now. *Today.*

Dirk slayed yet another of Olafsson's men, working his way through the melee.

Born of the same bloodline, their feud was ancient, and, at this point, no one was truly certain what had begun the feuds between the two factions to begin with. Only one thing stood out: land, which equaled power.

Dirk was descended of King Somerled, and as Lord of the Isles, he was allied to King Alexander III of Scotland. Morten

Olafsson, was descended from the rival Crovan dynasty, styling himself King of Mann and the Isles, and loyal to King Haakon of Norway. Needless to say, it made family gatherings non-existent. In fact, they were more prone to fighting for lands and power. Which Olafsson had taken to the extreme since the spring harvest.

Each of Dirk's twenty-nine years so far had been one battle after another. His father, Torquil and his grandfather, Beiste, had done all they could to try and unite the clans and remain loyal to their king. Moreover, they'd both died in great battles doing just that, and now it was up to Dirk to see their legacies continued.

Olafsson wanted what Dirk had. He sought to expand his empire, and in so doing, gain more power. But the only way to do it was to kill Dirk first, because Dirk wasn't going to bloody well hand it over. Not to that cruel whoreson. And killing Dirk? 'Twas a feat, his blackguard cousin had been attempting, and miserably failing at, for the past year. Olafsson was lucky that Dirk did not seek to return the favor. For he could. Tenfold. Despite being King of Mann and the Isles, Morten Olafsson had not developed near the amount of allies among the Scots. Many who felt threatened, simply paid their loyalty to Dirk, a blow that stung worse than any other, Dirk was certain. Now was a time for change. Starting with his blasted cousin's retreat.

Dirk simply wanted peace within his clan, for his people, and he didn't need his relation's lands to do it. Perhaps there was a way. If he could only strike some sort of treaty with the man that would put a satisfactory end to it all for both factions—one that didn't include either of them crossing over to the other side. Dirk would be eternally grateful if there was.

A man shoved him from behind, the jab of hardened steel scraping Dirk's spine. Thankfully, not the steel-tipped point, but rather the hilt of a sword. Dirk whirled around, kicking out and landing a blow on the other man's knee, the crunch of bone and cartilage lost in the melee. The Olafsson warrior cried out in pain, cursing as he stumbled backward. In his pain, he became wilder with his sword, waving it around seeking to hit anything he could with it—and achieving just that, all except for his mark, Dirk.

Dirk kicked again, saving his arm strength when his feet would do, and caught the man in his opposite knee. With both kneecaps crushed, the warrior collapsed, his sword slamming into the bloodied ground beside Dirk's feet. Dirk leapt back out of the way, then kicked once more, against the man's temple sending him down for good. He blocked a blow to his right, ducking another on his left and let his sword swing wide and hard to take one man and then another in a single swipe.

Known for his swordsmanship, not many wished to fight Dirk in a tourney, let alone a battle. Within seconds, he was once more cleaving a path toward his cousin, intent on ending this here, today. He marched forward with purpose, baring his teeth as blood ran in rivulets over his face and arms. The blood of his enemies.

Closer and closer he came to Morten, not so sure he wanted the man to retreat, but instead blood lust taking over. Perhaps it was time to once and for all show who was the more powerful of the two.

A dozen paces away now.

A young warrior, of perhaps twenty summers, leapt protectively in front of Olafsson, his face young and familiar.

Olafsson's son.

Dirk grimaced. One look at the lad and he knew he could easily take him down, like a spider pouncing on an insect stuck in his web. He'd cleave him in two. Take his head and declare it a victory, for killing the young warrior, his cousin's heir and pride, would put Olafsson in an early grave.

Why the hell had Olafsson brought the whelp?

As if seeing the thoughts ramble through Dirk's mind, Olafsson let out a mighty roar, loud enough that it echoed from the sword blades of every warrior.

Dirk raised his hand and issued his own answering cry, demanding the men put down their weapons, and within a heartbeat, all the fighting ceased. Men heaved labored breaths, blood covered them as though they'd all bathed in it, and swords momentarily fell to their sides.

Never in the history of battles had two enemies ceased fighting like this. Almost as if the warriors themselves were also tired of the constant. Battling for a prize that could not be won. The tension in the air was palpable.

The two cousins stared at each other. Hard, assessing glowers.

"I will kill him," Dirk said, his blade still at the lad's neck. "Else ye leave my land and take him with ye."

Olafsson's face remained placid, and the long pause was a disappointment to his son who must know his father was weighing the pros and cons of keeping him alive. "I will come back."

"Nay, ye willna." Dirk kept his voice calm and even. He had the upper hand, and he wasn't going to let it go. "Else, I hunt down your heir and kill him."

Olafsson flicked his gaze to his son and for a moment, Dirk thought he might make a sacrifice of his own child. Dirk had no children of his own, and for good reason, but if he did, he could never imagine that he'd even consider losing that child to gain power, for the child was the legacy. And Olafsson did not have any other sons to step into this one's place.

"Take your men and go," Dirk shouted, letting the tip of

his sword prick the lad's neck. "Swear to never come back to Dunstaffnage again. I will never let ye have my lands. I will die protecting them from your greedy paws. And no MacDougall to follow me will surrender."

Olafsson spit on the ground, his hands on his hips as he weighed his options but kept silent. The longer he remained uncommunicative, the more antsy the lad grew, in fact, he shifted his neck, causing Dirk's blade to pierce a little deeper. Blood trickled, bright red against the lad's pale white skin, and the glinting metal of Dirk's sword.

"Ye are killing your only heir," Dirk urged, his hand tightening on the hilt. "I'll not ask ye again."

Finally, Olafsson spit again and let out a nasty expletive. "I want something in return for surrendering."

Dirk hiked a brow and shook his head. "That is not how it works."

"A peace treaty." The man's gaze flicked to Dirk's blade at his son's neck. "Let him go. I'll negotiate."

"We talk in private," Dirk said.

The two leaders backed away from the warriors who in turn retreated to opposite ends of the battlefield, taking advantage of the reprieve to rest and clean their weapons.

"What do ye want?" Dirk pierced his sword in the dirt and crossed his arms over his chest. He might appear more relaxed, but in reality, he was poised to fight, and didn't trust his cousin at all.

"I want…" Olafsson stared at the bodies littering the moors. "I want a woman."

Dirk snorted. "Be serious."

Olafsson met his eyes. Damn, the man was serious. A glint of malice filled the dark depths. "I want your betrothed."

Dirk gritted his teeth, feeling insulted on behalf of a

woman who didn't exist. "I have no betrothed, and if I did, I'd be offended that ye'd even ask to have her."

The man grunted, his lip curling into a cruel semblance of a smile. "But for the price of peace?"

"I told ye I wasna going to give ye what is mine. What else?"

"I want what I came for," Olafsson growled.

Dirk cracked his neck and practiced an immeasurable amount of patience not to ram his head into his cousin's. "And I'm not going to give ye a damn thing. Leave us in peace and I willna harm your son."

"Not until I have something of yours."

The stubborn whoreson wouldn't leave it alone! "Why?" The question was simple, but Dirk didn't expect as simple an answer as he received.

"Should have been mine. My grandfather was the older son. All of this"—he swept his hands out—"should have been mind."

Dirk wanted to punch his *distant*, very distant, extremely removed, cousin in the face. The pure greed and bitterness came off him in nauseating waves. He fisted his hands beneath his arms, and ground his teeth so hard he was certain one would chip.

"I am not betrothed," Dirk said evenly, impressed it didn't come out a snarl. "I will not give ye my lands. If 'tis a woman ye want, I can give ye a MacDougall woman to wed." Even as he said it, he hated it. But one woman, a woman he didn't' know, could bring about the peace of all his people. Sacrifices had to be made. And he'd forever beg forgiveness of the lass' family "But if I hear one word of ye mistreating her, I will come for her, and I will bring pain and destruction to your lands."

Olafsson's lips pealed back from his teeth in a pathetic semblance of a smile. "Ye'll not get far, but ye'll not need to.

I'm in need of a wife, and more heirs, seeing as how I almost lost my only living son today. I will not harm the woman who is to bear my children."

Dirk nodded and reached forward to grip Olafsson's arm. "We will draw up the papers now and sign them before ye leave."

The man didn't return Dirk's extended reach. "She must be the most beautiful of your people. And intelligent."

"Aye," Dirk growled. "I'll make certain ye will be pleased."

At last, Olafsson reached for his arm, the blood of each other's men still slick on their skin as they grasped each other in a mutual show of agreement.

Within a few hours, the papers were signed, Olafsson's men were retreating and Dirk was burying his dead.

Despite having waged a treaty this day, guilt ate at him, souring his gut. He slugged back a dram of whisky, feeling it burn his insides. Today, he'd sold a woman. A woman he didn't even know, to a man he despised. He'd condemned some poor lass to a lifetime of misery.

All he could do to console himself was rationalize that her life would save hundreds and bring about years of peace. His people would understand. They would back him. And the lass would be grateful for being chosen as the only one who could save her people.

Sometimes sacrifices had to be made for peace.

CHAPTER TWO

～

*Castle Cameron*

COMMOTION FROM THE INNER BAILEY STARTLED LILIAS from where she'd been staring blankly at the mortar between the stones in the wall. *Riders.* The guards called out greetings. Horses huffed against the chinking of their tackle and their hooves clacked on the cobblestones.

Her body was heavy and her eyes still burned from the tears she'd shed. How was she going to stand to greet whomever it was that had come? All she wanted to do was curl up beside her mother and never let go. As much as she wanted to deny it, her mother, her pillar of strength, her champion, was dying. An affliction of the blood the physician said before he bled her and then left leaches to feed on her weakened body. A tumor growing in her mother's belly, the healer contradicted. Whichever it was, both the healer and the physician said it was not curable. They gave her tisanes to dull the pain, and broth because she could not eat whole foods.

Lilias's father and brother did not mourn as deeply, or visibly, as Lilias did, but she suspected that they had their own way of mourning that she wouldn't ever understand. Father was drinking more ale than usual, deep in his cups by supper time each night, shouting and ranting. And Rauld spent much more time in the village with the lassies, coming home late at night, reeking of debauchery.

And Lilias was left to pick up the pieces.

So, what was the point in greeting uninvited guests when the most important person in her world was lying at death's door?

"Go away," she whispered to the air, imagining her words somehow swirling out the window, and dropping like a bucket of cold water on whoever it was. Never mind that her mother would not have wanted that. Never mind that even though she lay weak, her mother was still making demands of Lilias from her bed. Demands like how to be the lady of the castle, that she had to be strong for her brother and father, and even know, Lilias could hear her mother's voice telling her to greet the strangers who'd come riding through their gates.

"My lady?" A guard stood in the doorway, his gaze leveled at her feet. "There are visitors here to see your mother. Your father directed me to find ye."

Lilias kept her voice disinterested, acting as though she'd not spent the last hour sobbing. "Who is it?"

"The ladies of MacDougall."

The ladies of MacDougall? Why on earth would they be calling on her? The Lord of Isles was the liege lord of her father, and for certes, her father had traveled to Dunstaffnage before, but never had Laird MacDougall come to Castle Cameron, nor had the ladies. Could they be coming to pay their respects to her mother? If that was the case, she couldn't deny them entry.

Lilias stood from her perch and swept her hands down the length of her skirts, smoothing out the wrinkles. "Please send them in."

As soon as the guard was gone, she used the cuffs of her sleeves to wipe at her face. She smoothed her hair and pinched her cheeks. But even that amount of primping, would not be able to hide the swollen, redness of her eyes.

A moment later, two women swept into the room dressed in fine wool arisaids made up of MacDougall colors of red, green and blue. One was a bit older than the other. The elder Lady MacDougall had auburn hair with streaks of gray, pulled into a tight braided circlet and skin that was still mostly smooth save for a few creases around her eyes, and mouth. One could only tell her advanced age, close to seventy summers, by the sharp points of bone where skin sagged. Her beauty was one that remained no matter her age, with noble bone structure, that gave her a classic elegance.

The younger lady was blonde, plump, and pretty. Perhaps nearing fifty summers. With smooth skin, creases at her watery blue eyes, she came off more kind and soft, than the older of the pair, who demanded respect and admiration.

"I am Lady Lilias," she said, introducing herself and sweeping into a curtsy.

"Rise, child," the older one said. "I am Lady Elle MacDougall, and this is my daughter-by-marriage, Lady Fenella, mother to the Laird of MacDougall, Lord of the Isles."

Lady Fenella offered a soft greeting.

"I am pleased to welcome ye to Castle Cameron. Please have a seat. Can I get ye some refreshment?"

Lady Fenella took the seat she was offered, but Lady Elle remained standing. "Aye, thank ye, my lady. Refreshments would be nice as the roads were rather dusty. We've come to speak with your mother."

"Please do sit." Lilias swept her hand toward a carved, oak chair that her mother used to occupy. "I've only just finished with that cushion, and I would be honored if ye were the first to sit in it."

Lady Elle examined the crimson finches embroidered on the cushion, with a smile that softened her briskness. She sat down, and folded her hands in her lap.

"My mother has been ill of late." Lilias informed a servant in the corridor that refreshments were needed for their guests before she took a seat opposite the two ladies. "I hope ye dinna mind speaking to me instead."

"Of course not. In fact," Lady Elle smiled again, her demeanor engaging. "Ye were the verra reason we've come."

"Me?" Lilias tried to hide her surprise, but it didn't work.

"Aye." Lady Elle nodded, squinting as she examined Lilias. "Your beauty and wit have reached many within the land."

Lilias swallowed hard, uncertain how to respond other

than to say, "Thank ye." How had her beauty and wit reached the MacDougalls? *Oh, zounds*! Were they here to suggest… that she… wed the MacDougall? Her heart dropped to her feet and she felt the color draining from her face. She was not ready to wed. Did not want to leave her ailing mother. And her father and brother needed her. Who else would keep the books or tend to the needs of the castle and their people?

"Ye need not be nervous, lass," Lady Fenella put in.

"Have ye heard of the treaty?" Lady Elle asked, jumping right into the heart of the mysterious matter.

Lilias shook her head, still trying to figure out where her stomach had gone and why her fingers were now going numb. She wasn't certain she wanted to know about the treaty. Nay, she was definitely certain she didn't want to know.

"Laird MacDougall and Morten Olafsson came to an agreement of peace on the battlefield, on one condition," Lady Elle explained.

The lady paused as she, and her daughter-by-marriage, were served a cup of watered wine by a servant, and a bowl of sweetened almonds.

"The condition?" Lilias urged, wringing her hands in her lap and waving the servant away. In fact, she wanted to jump up and sweep all the refreshments away and demand they stop their dillydallying and tell her right away what was going on.

"The condition was that my grandson needed to find a wife for Morten Olafsson. One of superior beauty, intelligence and wit."

Lady Fenella smiled, speaking around several almonds. "We have been to interview many eligible maidens."

Morten Olafsson. King of Mann and the Isles. The man who was constantly bringing war to their lands. The enemy of her people. A man her brother and father had fought against on behalf of Laird MacDougall.

They wanted to test *her* in regards to marrying that... that... that *blackguard*? Angry heat flushed up her neck to burn her eyes.

"And now ye've come here?" Lilias was unable to keep the incredulity from her tone. "Am I to be paraded with the other lassies as chattel?" Voice sharp, she winced at having spoken so to women that were clearly of a higher rank than she, but how could it be helped?

Oh, if her mother were in the room... She'd have given Lilias such a sharp pinch! *Grateful*, that was what her mother would say, *be grateful*. A great honor. A magnificent prospect. *Bah! Rubbish!* This was horrible.

A moment ago she'd been contemplating a life without her mother, and then the next thing she knew, two women had burst into her life telling her she was possibly to marry a complete stranger, one whom was rumored to be a monster, in order to settle the peace in their land. Aye, she could fall to the floor now and not get up.

"My dear, I understand that this is very unnerving," Lady Fenella said softly.

"Unnerving?" Lilias cut her off, jumping to her feet. "I believe it is folly. Please, I dinna mean to be rude, but ye've come to the wrong place. I willna do it." Her mind went back to the time her mother had taken her to see the *taibhsear* as a child. This was not the prophecy. This was not what she'd thought to happen.

Of course, she'd kept her eyes wide since she'd been a wee thing for a man as the seer had described. Dark of hair, stormy of eye, fiercer than a gale storm, but never had she come across a man such as that. And now, if she were to be tossed into the ring with a bevy of other lassies, she might never see the prophecy come true. And then what would she have left of her mother?

Lady Cameron had been ill for many months, and the only thing that seemed to keep her holding on was that she wanted to see Lilias married off to whoever the man was that the seer had envisioned.

"I canna. I willna." Lilias started for the door.

"Lass, please." Lady Elle's voice was soft, calm, drawing Lilias back when she wanted to run from the solar. "I know this is upsetting news. I would not want this for myself, either. And I do understand feeling as though ye have no control over your own future. But, consider the alternatives."

"Which are?" Lilias scrutinized the older of the two women. The silver streaks of color glinted in her auburn hair, and the lines around her mouth showed she smiled often. That she was happy. Lilias wanted to be happy.

"My grandson has decreed that any woman being inter-viewed who will not cooperate is to be... imprisoned." Lady Fenella shot her an imploring gaze.

"Imprisoned?" Lilias's heart did a flip. She shook her head.

"Does my father know what ye've come to discuss with me?"

Lady Fenella nodded while Lady Elle kept her gazed locked on Lilias. "He was presented with the document."

"The document?"

"The orders from my son, his overlord," Lady Fenella said. "Please sit back down. I'd hate for your father to be taken by our guards." So it would seem, despite her kind affect, the woman did have more mettle than Lilias previously imagined.

"Taken?" Lilias's feet moved back toward her chair of their own accord and she sank onto the suddenly uncom-fortable cushion. So, this was how it would be.

"Lady Lilias, we need to do this. We despise it just as much as ye do. Please dinna resist us." Lady Fenella reached forward to pat Lilias's hand.

Vision blurring, Lilias felt herself nodding, as thought self-preservation had taken control of her body and mind.

"Before your mother was taken ill, did she teach ye the managing of a household?" Lady Elle sipped at her wine as if waiting to hear a tale.

"Aye." With a numb tongue, Lilias listed off the things she did on a daily basis within her father's castle, including how she tended to the people in their village.

"And can ye read or write?" Lady Elle asked.

Lilias hesitated to answer. A woman was not supposed to read or write, it was considered undignified. Well, that gave her an idea. If she told the truth—which was that she could—then perhaps they would find her unworthy of marriage to the Olafsson wretch. She'd do anything to be found lacking as a good wife. So, she nodded.

The two women raised a brow and exchanged a meaningful look. That had to be a good sign, right?

"What of arithmetic?" Was that a hint of a shudder she saw in Lady Fenella's shoulders?

Lilias smiled. Her plan was working. "Aye. I studied with my brother's tutor." She sat up straighter. "And, I've kept my father's books, though he and my brother both believe it is themselves." *Ah-ha*! The nail in the coffin. They would certainly not want her now. She was too smart, and boastful. A lord could never desire a woman who might be smarter than himself.

Lady Elle raised her brow in challenge. "Show us."

Lilias leapt at the opportunity. She went to the seat before the window and opened the trunk beneath it, pulling out a leather-bound book. It was filled with parchment, a journal her tutor had made for her. She opened it up, her fingers sliding over the scrawled words she'd written as a youth.

She read to them from the first pages.

*"Birds let out their high-pitched call,*
*Signaling of danger to one and all.*
*I am not danger, I shout my plea.*
*I am freedom, and freedom is we.*
*To soar, to sing, to perch, to live,*
*To despair, to love, to lose, to give.*
*I am the wind, the light of the sun.*
*I am courage, and together we're one."*

When she finished reading, she held it out for Lady Elle to see.

Lady Elle gazed on her with an expression Lilias couldn't quite place. 'Twas a mixture of suspicion and admiration.

Lilias straightened her shoulders, wishing she'd not bared her soul to these women. It had been impulsive. A need to show them she had talent, but that she also possessed a deeper soul than most, that what they had planned would suffocate her. Kill her. That a man like Olafsson wouldn't want her for a wife.

Her plan looked to be backfiring.

"Did ye write this?" Lady Elle asked.

Lilias drew in a breath through her nose, and then expelled it slowly before answering. "Aye."

"'Tis beautiful, lass. Full of heart." Lady Fenella eyed her with a weighty expression, as though seeing her for what she truly was.

"Thank ye," Lilias said, a prickle of pride nudging its way through her fear.

"Is this how ye envision yourself?" Lady Elle asked. "Free? Courageous?"

Lilias bit the inside of her cheek, afraid they might laugh at her as her nursemaid had when she'd read it, for how could a woman ever think of herself as thus? "'Tis about birds, nothing more."

Lady Elle's mouth quirked in a smile. "Now we both know that is not so."

Lilias didn't answer, instead jutting her chin forward in defiance. She'd not admit the truth. What did it matter to them what her poem meant? What did it matter to them that she thought of herself as that bird? That she wanted to soar through the air, to be free, to be courageous? They wouldn't understand anyway, they were here to put her in a shallow grave. For that was what marriage to a stranger in a strange land would be.

Lady Fenella piped up then, interrupting Lilias and momentarily startling her from her internal thoughts. "And let us say there are eighty-five villagers who need to pay a tax of eighteen pounds each, what should ye expect the sum total tax to be collected?"

Lilias worked the numbers in her head as she'd done since she was a lass. "One thousand five hundred and thirty."

Lady Fenella looked to Lady Elle who nodded. "Ye didna need a slate to work out the numbers." 'Twas a statement rather than a question.

Lilias squared her shoulders. "I've not needed a slate for many years."

"Can ye sing?" Lady Fenella asked, a smile brightening her youthful face. "And dance?"

"Play an instrument?" Lady Elle added.

Lilias nodded. "But I dinna feel the muse this morn."

Lady Elle laughed. "Ye're not a minstrel, ye've not the luxury of traveling from town to town, striking up a song when the muse deems it right. Ye're a lady. And a lady must entertain her husband when he asks. Now, sing me a song. Play that harp, too." She pointed to the small harp set in the corner of the solar.

Trudging with heavy feet, Lilias picked up the harp and carried it back toward her chair.

"I do so love harp music." Lady Fenella sighed into her cup.

Lilias closed her eyes, and pretended it was her mother sitting before her. That she was singing the song of the fairies for her sweet Mama, and that her mother was dancing before her as she'd done before she'd taken ill. All the sadness, the fear, the hope she felt came through that song. The sorrow of her mother's illness, the two MacDougall ladies, the impending inspection, all of it disappeared. And when she was finished, she shook herself as if from a daze.

"Lovely, dear. Simply lovely," Lady Elle said. "Take us to your mother now."

Lilias's fingers stilled on the harp, her jaw tightening. "My mother is ill. She is not seeing guests. I do apologize for having to disappoint ye on that account."

"I would like to speak with her," Lady Elle said as though Lilias hadn't spoken at all.

"I'm afraid she's taking a rest—"

But anything more Lilias might have said was cut short by the solar door inching open and her mother standing there in her linen chemise, bare toes and a fur wrap over her shoulders. She looked so small standing there. So frail. Cheekbones jutted from beneath her pale skin. Not at all the formidable woman she'd once been.

Lilias felt herself choking up, but quickly regained her senses as she ran to her mother. "Mama, what are ye doing out of bed?"

"I heard ye playing, love. Ye know I like that song. Who are these ladies?" Lady Cameron's shoulders stiffened, bringing her stooped shoulders back as she transformed into the lady of the castle, somehow managing to maintain an air of authority over their guests.

Before Lilias could introduce them, Lady Elle stepped forward. "I am Lady Elle MacDougall, and this is my daughter-by-marriage, Lady Fenella."

"To what do we owe this honor?" her mother asked, her eyes narrowing. She flicked her gaze to Lilias, but the question in her eyes, Lilias wasn't sure how to answer.

Did her mother know of the treaty?

"We came on behest of my son," Lady Fenella said. "And the treaty he has made with Morten Olafsson, King of Mann and the Isles."

"I've heard of the treaty," her mother said, surprising Lilias. "But what does it have to do with my daughter?"

"We," the two women exchanged a glance, "have decided that your daughter shall be presented to the MacDougall warriors as a possible candidate in the treaty, to wed Morten Olafsson."

"The prophecy," her mother murmured, her knees buckling.

"Mama, nay," Lilias said reaching out to steady her. "I must get ye back to bed."

Her mother nodded, then said to Lady Elle, "Come with me. Tell me everything."

Lady Cameron shooed away Lilias's complaints and told her to go downstairs with Lady Fenella to see the guardsmen outside.

Dutifully, she followed. Dutifully, she turned in a circle and sang for the twelve men as they stared her down. Dutifully she gave over her soul to the devil.

But inside, she seethed.

*Want to read more? Check out **Laird of Twilight** available now!*

# EXCERPT FROM THE HIGHLANDER'S GIFT

*An injured Warrior...*

Betrothed to a princess until she declares his battle wound
has incapacitated him as a man, Sir Niall Oliphant is glad to
step aside and let the spoiled royal marry his brother. He's
more than content to fade into the background with his
injuries and remain a bachelor forever, until he meets the
Earl of Sutherland's daughter, a lass more beautiful than any
other, a lass who makes him want to stand up and fight
again.

*A lady who won't let him fail...*
As daughter of one of the most powerful earls and Highland chieftains in Scotland, Bella Sutherland can marry anyone she wants—but she doesn't want a husband. When she spies an injured warrior at the Yule festival who has been shunned by the Bruce's own daughter, she decides a husband in name only might be her best solution.

They both think they're agreeing to a marriage of convenience, but love and fate has other plans...

CHAPTER ONE

～

*Dupplin Castle*
*Scottish Highlands*
*Winter, 1318*

Sir Niall Oliphant had lost something.

Not a trinket, or a boot. Not a pair of hose, or even his favorite mug. Nothing as trivial as that. In fact, he wished it *was* so minuscule that he could simply replace it. What'd he'd lost was devastating, and yet it felt entirely selfish given some of those closest to him had lost their lives.

He was still here, living and breathing. He was still walking around on his own two feet. Still handsome in the face. Still able to speak coherently, even if he didn't want to.

But he couldn't replace what he'd lost.

What he'd lost would irrevocably change his life, his entire future. It made him want to back into the darkest corner and let his life slip away, to forget about even having a future at all. To give everything he owned to his brother and say goodbye. He was useless now. Unworthy.

Niall cleared the cobwebs that had settled in his throat by slinging back another dram of whisky. The shutters in his darkened bedchamber were closed tight, the fire long ago grown cold. He didn't allow candles in the room, nor visitors. So when a knock sounded at his door, he ignored it, preferring to chug his spirits from the bottle rather than pouring it into a cup.

The knocking grew louder, more insistent.

"Go away," he bellowed, slamming the whisky down on the side table beside where he sat, and hearing the clay jug shatter. A shard slid into his finger, stinging as the liquor splashed over it. But he didn't care.

This pain, pain in his only index finger, he wanted to have. Wanted a reminder there was still some part of him left. Part of him that could still feel and bleed. He tried to ignore that part of him that wanted to be alive, however small it was.

The handle on the door rattled, but Niall had barred it the day before. Refusing anything but whisky. Maybe he could drink himself into an oblivion he'd never wake from. Then all of his worries would be gone forever.

"Niall, open the bloody door."

The sound of his brother's voice through the cracks had Niall's gaze widening slightly. Walter was a year younger than he was. And still whole. Walter had tried to understand Niall's struggle, but what man could who'd not been through it himself?

"I said go away, ye bloody whoreson." His words slurred, and he went to tipple more of the liquor only to recall he'd just shattered it everywhere.

*Hell and damnation.* The only way to get another bottle would be to open the door.

"I'll pretend I didna hear ye just call our dear mother a whore. Open the damned door, or I'll take an axe to it."

Like hell he would. Walter was the least aggressive one in their family. Sweet as a lad, he'd grown into a strong warrior, but he was also known as the heart of the Oliphant clan. The idea of him chopping down a door was actually funny. Outside, the corridor grew silent, and Niall leaned his head back against the chair, wondering how long he had until his brother returned, and if it was enough time to sneak down to the cellar and get another jug of whisky.

Needless to say, when a steady thwacking sounded at the door—reminding Niall quite a bit like the heavy side of an axe—he sat up straighter and watched in drunken fascination as the door started to splinter. Shards of wood came flying through the air as the hole grew larger and the sound of the axe beating against the surface intensified.

Walter had grown some bloody ballocks.

Incredible.

Didn't matter. What would Walter accomplish by breaking down the door? What could he hope would happen?

Niall wasn't going to leave the room or accept food.

Niall wasn't going to move on with his life.

So he sat back and waited, curious more than anything as to what Walter's plan would be once he'd gained entry.

Just as tall and broad of shoulder as Niall, Walter kicked through the remainder of the door and ducked through the ragged hole.

"That's enough." Walter looked down at Niall, his face fierce, reminding him very much of their father when they were lads.

"That's enough?" Niall asked, trying to keep his eyes wide

but having a hard time. The light from the corridor gave his brother a darkened, shadowy look.

"Ye've sat in this bloody hell hole for the past three days." Walter gestured around the room. "Ye stink of shite. Like a bloody pig has laid waste to your chamber."

"Are ye calling me a shite pig?" Niall thought about standing up, calling his brother out, but that seemed like too much effort.

"Mayhap I am. Will it make ye stand up any faster?"

Niall pursed his lips, giving the impression of actually considering it. "Nay."

"That's what I thought. But I dinna care. Get up."

Niall shook his head slowly. "I'd rather not."

"I'm not asking."

*My, my.* Walter's ballocks were easily ten times than Niall had expected. The man was bloody testing him to be sure.

"Last time I checked, I was the eldest," Niall said.

"Ye might have been born first, but ye lost your mind some time ago, which makes me the better fit for making decisions."

Niall hiccupped. "And what decisions would ye be making, wee brother?"

"Getting your arse up. Getting ye cleaned up. Airing out the gongheap."

"Doesna smell so bad in here." Niall gave an exaggerated sniff, refusing to admit that Walter was indeed correct. It smelled horrendous.

"I'm gagging, brother. I might die if I have to stay much longer."

"Then by all means, pull up a chair."

"Ye're an arse."

"No more so than ye."

"Not true."

Niall sighed heavily. "What do ye want? Why would ye make me leave? I've nothing to live for anymore."

"Ye've eight-thousand reasons to live, ye blind goat."

"Eight thousand?"

"A random number." Walter waved his hand and kicked at something on the floor. "Ye've the people of your clan, the warriors ye lead, your family. The woman ye're betrothed to marry. Everyone is counting on ye, and ye must come out of here and attend to your duties. Ye've mourned long enough."

"How can ye presume to tell me that I've mourned long enough? Ye know nothing." A slow boiling rage started in Niall's chest. All these men telling him how to feel. All these men thinking they knew better. A bunch of bloody ballocks!

"Aye, I've not lost what ye have, brother. Ye're right. I dinna know what 'tis like to be ye, either. But I know what 'tis like to be the one down in the hall waiting for ye to come and take care of your business. I know what 'tis like to look upon the faces of the clan as they worry about whether they'll be raided or ravaged while their leader sulks in a vat of whisky and does nothing to care for them."

Niall gritted his teeth. No one understood. And he didn't need the reminder of his constant failings.

"Then take care of it," Niall growled, jerking forward fast enough that his vision doubled. "Ye've always wanted to be first. Ye've always wanted what was mine. Go and have it. Have it all."

Walter took a step back as though Niall had hit him. "How can ye say that?" Even in the dim light, Niall could see the pain etched on his brother's features. Aye, what he'd said was a lie, but it had made him feel better all the same.

"Ye heard me. Get the fuck out." Niall moved to push himself from the chair, remembered too late how difficult that would be, and fell back into it. Instead, he let out a string of curses that had Walter shaking his head.

"Ye need to get yourself together, decide whether or not ye are going to turn your back on this clan. Do it for yourself. Dinna go down like this. Ye are still Sir Niall fucking Oliphant. Warrior. Heir to the chiefdom of Oliphant. Hero. Leader. Brother. Soon to be husband and father."

Walter held his gaze unwaveringly. A torrent of emotion jabbed from that dark look into Niall's chest, crushing his heart.

"Get out," he said again through gritted teeth, feeling the pain of rejecting his brother acutely.

They'd always been so close. And even though he was pushing him away, he also desperately wanted to pull him closer.

He wanted to hug him tightly, to tell him not to worry, that soon enough he'd come out of the dark and be the man Walter once knew. But those were all lies, for he would never be the same again, and he couldn't see how he would ever be able to exit this room and attempt a normal life.

"Ye're not the only one who's lost a part of himself," Walter muttered as he ducked beneath the door. "I want my brother back."

"Your brother is dead."

At that, Walter paused. He turned back around, a snarl poised on his lips, and Niall waited longingly for whatever insult would come out. Any chance to engage in a fight, but then Walter's face softened. "Maybe he is."

With those soft words uttered, he disappeared, leaving behind the gaping hole and the shattered wood on the floor, a haunting mirror image to the wide-open wound Niall felt in his soul.

Niall glanced down to his left, at the sleeve that hung empty at his side, a taunting reminder of his failure in battle. Warrior. Ballocks! Not even close.

When he considered lying down on the ground and

licking the whisky from the floor, he knew it was probably time to leave his chamber. But he was no good to anyone outside of his room. Perhaps he could prove that fact once and for all, then Walter would leave him be. And he knew his brother spoke the truth about smelling like a pig. He'd not bathed in days. If he was going to prove he was worthless as a leader now, he would do so smelling decent, so people took him seriously rather than believing him to be mad.

Slipping through the hole in the door, he walked noise-lessly down the corridor to the stairs at the rear used by the servants, tripping only once along the way. He attempted to steal down the winding steps, a feat that nearly had him breaking his neck. In fact, he took the last dozen steps on his arse. Once he reached the entrance to the side of the bailey, he lifted the bar and shoved the door open, the cool wind a welcome blast against his heated skin. With the sun set, no one saw him creep outside and slink along the stone as he made his way to the stables and the massive water trough kept for the horses. He might as well bathe there, like the animal he was.

Trough in sight, he staggered forward and tumbled head-first into the icy water.

Niall woke sometime later, still in the water, but turned over at least. He didn't know whether to be grateful he'd not drowned. His clothes were soaked, and his legs hung out on either side of the wooden trough. It was still dark, so at least he'd not slept through the night in the chilled water.

He leaned his head back, body covered in wrinkled gooseflesh and teeth chattering, and stared up at the sky. Stars dotted the inky-black landscape and swaths of clouds streaked across the moon, as if one of the gods had swiped his hand through it, trying to wipe it away. But the moon was steadfast. Silver and bright and ever present. Returning as it should each night, though hiding its beauty day after day until it was just a sliver that made one wonder if it would return.

What was he doing out here? Not just in the tub freezing his idiot arse off, but here in this world? Why hadn't he been taken? Why had only part of him been stolen? Cut away…

Niall shuddered, more from the memory of that moment when his enemy's sword had cut through his armor, skin, muscle and bone. The crunching sound. The incredible pain.

He squeezed his eyes shut, forcing the memories away.

This is how he'd been for the better part of four months. Stumbling drunk and angry about the castle when he wasn't holed up in his chamber. Yelling at his brother, glowering at his father and mother, snapping at anyone who happened to cross his path. He'd become everything he hated.

There had been times he'd thought about ending it all. He always came back to the simple question that was with him now as he stared up at the large face of the moon.

"Why am I still here?" he murmured.

"Likely because ye havena pulled your arse out of the bloody trough."

*Walter.*

Niall's gaze slid to the side to see his brother standing there, arms crossed over his chest. "Are ye my bloody shadow? Come to tell me all my sins?"

"When will ye see I'm not the enemy? I want to help."

Niall stared back up at the moon, silently asking what he should do, begging for a sign.

Walter tugged at his arm. "Come on. Get out of the trough. Ye're not a pig as much as ye've been acting the part. Let us get ye some food."

Niall looked over at his little brother, perhaps seeing him for the first time. His throat felt tight, closing in on itself as a well of emotion overflowed from somewhere deep in his gut.

"Why do ye keep trying to help me? All I've done is berate ye for it."

"Aye. That's true, but I know ye speak from pain. Not from your heart."

"I dinna think I have a heart left."

Walter rolled his eyes and gave a swift tug, pulling him halfway from the trough. Though Niall was weak from lack of food and too much whisky, he managed to get himself the rest of the way out. He stood in the moonlight, dripping water around the near frozen ground.

"Ye have a heart. Ye have a soul. One arm. That is all ye've lost. Ye still have your manhood, aye?"

Niall shrugged. Aye, he still had his bloody cock, but what woman wanted a decrepit man heaving overtop of her with his mangled body in full view.

"I know what ye're thinking," Walter said. "And the answer is, every eligible maiden and all her friends. Not to mention the kitchen wenches, the widows in the glen, and their sisters."

"Ballocks," Niall muttered.

"Ye're still handsome. Ye're still heir to a powerful clan. Wake up, man. This is not ye. Ye canna let the loss of your arm be the destruction of your whole life. Ye're not the first man to ever be maimed in battle. Dinna be a martyr."

"Says the man with two arms."

"Ye want me to cut it off? I'll bloody do it." Walter turned in a frantic circle as if looking for the closest thing with a sharp edge.

Niall narrowed his eyes, silent, watching, waiting. When had his wee brother become such an intense force? Walter marched toward the barn, hand on the door, yanked it wide as if to continue the blockhead search. Niall couldn't help following after his brother who marched forward with purpose, disappearing inside the barn.

A flutter of worry dinged in Niall's stomach. Walter wouldn't truly go through with something so stupid, would he?

When he didn't immediately reappear, Niall's pang of worry heightened into dread. Dammit, he just might. With all the changes Walter had made recently, there was every possibility that he'd gone mad. Well, Niall might wish to disappear, but not before he made certain his brother was all right.

With a groan, Niall lurched forward, grabbed the door and yanked it open. The stables were dark and smelled of horses, leather and hay. He could hear a few horses nickering, and the soft snores of the stable hands up on the loft fast asleep.

"Walter," he hissed. "Enough. No more games."

Still, there was silence.

He stepped farther into the barn, and the door closed behind him, blocking out all the light save for a few strips that sank between cracks in the roof.

His feet shuffled silently on the dirt floor. Where the bloody hell had his brother gone?

And why was his heart pounding so fiercely? He trudged toward the first set of stables, touching the wood of the gates. A horse nudged his hand with its soft muzzle, blowing out a soft breath that tickled his palm, and Niall's heart squeezed.

"Prince," he whispered, leaning his forehead down until he felt it connect with the warm, solidness of his warhorse. Prince nickered and blew out another breath.

Niall had not ridden in months. If not for his horse, he might be dead. But rather than be irritated Prince had done his job, he felt nothing but pride that the horse he'd trained from a colt into a mammoth had done his duty.

After Niall's arm had been severed and he was left for dead, Prince had nudged him awake, bent low and nipped at

Niall's legs until he'd managed to crawl and heave himself belly first over the saddle. Prince had taken him home like that, a bleeding sack of grain.

Having thought him dead, the clan had been shocked and surprised to see him return, and that's when the true battle for his life had begun. He'd lost so much blood, succumbed to fever, and stopped breathing more than once. Hell, it was a miracle he was still alive.

Which begged the question—*why, why, why...*

"He's missed ye." Walter was beside him, and Niall jerked toward his brother, seeing his outline in the dark.

"Is that why ye brought me in here?"

"Did ye really think I'd cut off my arm?" Walter chuckled. "Ye know I like to fondle a wench and drink at the same time."

Niall snickered. "Ye're an arse."

"Aye, 'haps I am."

They were silent for a few minutes, Niall deep in thought as he stroked Prince's soft muzzle. His mind was a torment of unanswered questions. "Walter, I...I dinna know what to do."

"Take it one day at a time, brother. But do take it. No more being locked in your chamber."

Niall nodded even though his brother couldn't see him. A phantom twinge of pain rippled through the arm that was no longer there, and he stopped himself from moving to rub the spot, not wanting to humiliate himself in front of his brother. When would those pains go away? When would his body realize his arm had long since become bone in the earth?

One day at a time. That was something he might be able to do. "I'll have bad days."

"Aye. And good ones, too."

Niall nodded. He longed to saddle Prince and go for a ride but realized he wasn't even certain how to mount with only one arm to grab hold of the saddle. "I have so much to learn."

"Aye. But as I recall, ye're a fast learner."

"I'll start training again tomorrow."

"Good."

"But I willna be laird. Walter, the right to rule is yours now."

"Ye've time before ye need to make that choice. Da is yet breathing and making a ruckus."

"Aye. But I want ye to know what's coming. No matter what, I canna do that. I have to learn to pull on my bloody shirt first."

Walter slapped him on the back and squeezed his shoulder. "The lairdship is yours, with or without a shirt. Only thing I want is my brother back."

Niall drew in a long, mournful breath. "I'm not sure he's coming back. Ye'll have to learn to deal with me, the new me."

"New ye, old ye, still *ye.*"

Want to read the rest of *The Highlander's Gift*?

# ABOUT THE AUTHOR

Eliza Knight is an award-winning and *USA Today* bestselling author of over fifty sizzling historical romance and erotic romance. Under the name E. Knight, she pens rip-your-heart-out historical fiction. While not reading, writing or researching for her latest book, she chases after her three children. In her spare time (if there is such a thing…) she likes daydreaming, wine-tasting, traveling, hiking, staring at the stars, watching movies, shopping and visiting with family and friends. She lives atop a small mountain with her own knight in shining armor, three princesses and two very naughty puppies. Visit Eliza at http://www.elizaknight.com or her historical blog History Undressed: www.historyundressed.com. Sign up for her newsletter to get news about books, events, contests and sneak peaks! http://eepurl.com/CSFFD

facebook.com/elizaknightfiction

twitter.com/elizaknight

instagram.com/elizaknightfiction

bookbub.com/authors/eliza-knight

goodreads.com/elizaknight

# MORE BOOKS BY ELIZA KNIGHT

THE SUTHERLAND LEGACY

*The Highlander's Gift*
  *The Highlander's Quest — in the Ladies of the Stone anthology*

PIRATES OF BRITANNIA: DEVILS OF THE DEEP

*Savage of the Sea*
*The Sea Devil*
*A Pirate's Bounty*

THE STOLEN BRIDE SERIES

*The Highlander's Temptation*
*The Highlander's Reward*
*The Highlander's Conquest*
*The Highlander's Lady*
*The Highlander's Warrior Bride*

THE HIGHLAND BOUND SERIES (EROTIC TIME-TRAVEL)

*Behind the Plaid*
*Bared to the Laird*
*Dark Side of the Laird*
*Highlander's Touch*
*Highlander Undone*
*Highlander Unraveled*

WICKED WOMEN

*Her Desperate Gamble*
*Seducing the Sheriff*
*Kiss Me, Cowboy*

∾

UNDER THE NAME E. KNIGHT

TALES FROM THE TUDOR COURT

*My Lady Viper*
*Prisoner of the Queen*

ANCIENT HISTORICAL FICTION

*A Day of Fire: a novel of Pompeii*
*A Year of Ravens: a novel of Boudica's Rebellion*

Made in United States
North Haven, CT
05 January 2022

14145163R00145